BEECHER

BOOKS BY DAN McCALL

The Example of Richard Wright

The Man Says Yes

Jack the Bear

Beecher

Dan McCall

BEECHER

a novel

TC
THOMAS CONGDON BOOKS

E. P. Dutton · NEW YORK

For information contact:
E.P. Dutton, 2 Park Avenue,
New York, N.Y. 10016

Library of Congress Cataloging in Publication Data
McCall, Dan.
Beecher.
"Thomas Congdon Books."
1. Beecher, Henry Ward, 1813–1887, in fiction,
drama, poetry, etc. 2. Beecher, Thomas Kinnicut,
1824–1900—Fiction. I. Title.
PZ4.M12217Be [PS3563.A257] 813'.5'4 79–12358

ISBN: 0-525-06215-7

Published simultaneously in Canada by
Clarke, Irwin & Company Limited
Toronto & Vancover
Designed by Nicola Mazzella

10 9 8 7 6 5 4 3 2 1

First Edition

This book is for David

I acknowledge with gratitude the generous support of the American Council of Learned Societies. For essential help in research, my thanks to the American Antiquarian Society and to the university libraries of Yale, Harvard, Radcliffe College, the United States Military Academy at West Point, and Cornell. Of all the books on the Beechers, five proved invaluable to me: Constance Rourke's *Trumpets of Jubilee,* William G. McLoughlin's *The Meaning of Henry Ward Beecher,* Robert Shaplen's *Free Love and Heavenly Sinners,* Clifford E. Clark, Jr.'s *Henry Ward Beecher,* and Marie Caskey's *Chariot of Fire.* The official, three-thousand-page transcript of the great trial in Brooklyn City Court is *Theodore Tilton vs. Henry Ward Beecher, Action for Criminal Connection* (McDivitt, Campbell & Co., 1875).

D. Mc.

BEECHER

The first thing this rough-
neck preacher from out there in Indianapolis did,
when he answered the call to Brooklyn's Plymouth
Church, was remove the pulpit. And install a throne.

The great Congregational edifice goes straighta-
way through from Orange to Pineapple (the very
street names testifying to the pastor's mania for
horticulture). In the massive central sanctuary, one
hundred five feet by eighty feet, the pews are
arranged in a vast semi-circle, with plush red velvet
cushions, two thousand one hundred places—and
another one thousand in chairs, benches, gallery,
and standing room—all centering on his throne. He
extended a platform, a kind of runway out into the
semi-circle; he said, "It is perfect—because it is
built on a principle—the principle of social and

personal magnetism, emanating reciprocally." Henry Ward Beecher—my big brother, my half-brother—talks that way.

His house is a big brownstone at 124 Columbia Heights, two blocks from the church. In Henry's parlor there are three Persian rugs, one on top of the other, because there is no place else to put them and he could not resist buying them. The fun of his life is sneaking the stuff into the house without his wife noticing him. A mischievous boy. Yet our sister Isabella tells me (Isabella tells everything) that Henry once groaned to her, "I dread to go back to my own house." At Plymouth Church there is an abundance of tears, laughter, and cheering. At his own house there is his wife, Eunice. Her silence is not peace and quiet.

So Henry likes to cheat on her by pretending to give her all the money, while he is forever running out of cash. He has filled their house to overflowing with things: little trays, tiny jars, vases, enameled sweetmeat boxes, porcelains, Venetian and Bohemian glass, silken scarves, embroidered cushions, plushy carpets, velvet drapes. Indeed, my brother has a collection of stuffed birds of paradise; this morning, still huffing from the ferry-boat, I spent some time studying one of the more macabre specimens, until the bird's lambent eye stared me down. And, of course, Henry is infamous for his "color-opiates," as he calls them, the unset gems that he carries with him—amethysts, sapphires, topazes, and (his special favorites) opals; he will sit in a large chair and roll those gems in his hands or sweat out a sermon at a table, staring at a scatter of them for inspiration. Perhaps his mania is merely part of a national clamor for sumptuous decoration, our

American roar for luxury. Or I should see it more generously—as some kind of release from Henry's bitter pauper days out in Ohio and Indiana. Henry himself sees it that way and grumbles about Eunice: "In Indianapolis she hated our poverty; in Brooklyn she hates our prosperity." But I can never pitch myself headlong into the meaning of it when I am simply trying to keep ahold of myself amidst the chaos of bric-a-brac, the clutter of bone china, intricate salt cellars, exquisite cut-glass pitchers and bowls, crystal goblets, heavy silver with inlay initials, a royal spread on a double-damask cloth. This very morning, before church, under bronze ornaments hanging in a splatter of autumn leaves, we turn into absolute heathens—Spanish mackerel and coffee.

How, I wonder, as I often do, how could an outsider know what a family like ours feels like? With ten surviving siblings now (though Isabella, Jamesy, and I are "the other Beechers," the children of Father and Harriet Porter, not the great brood, not the prize stock of Father and Roxana Foote), we are all marooned in a constant changing of allegiances, fierce defiance, and unyielding loyalty, a dreadful grinding on the nervous system. Especially when we gather here, at Henry's house, with all the spouses and rowdy kin, it is an endless bumping into Time. At the table I watch alone while brother Charley argues with sister Mary. I exchange a glance with sister Catharine, for we both have seen sister Isabella shoot the butter straight into her lap, then daintily dribble nectar on her bosom, and fairly die with the horror of being confined in a single, human, female form. I do not meet my brother Edward's eyes across the table because I was so devoted to Edward once, and I know he is a good man, but I do so distrust him, and the thunder booms in my head because Edward has not met my eyes, because he knows I was so devoted to him, he knows he is a good man, and it wasn't his fault that I became a freshman at Illinois College when he was President of Illinois College (he only got the Presidency as a consolation prize for the Professorship at Dartmouth that he coveted). But when I went to Illinois to study under Edward, all he could say was that he was forced to live "in sucker style, where everybody is shaking so hard with the durn ague, they can't find time to die." Edward is a sour man, a study in thwarted ambition; even in our own family he is treated as a baroque curiosity. And now he has lost a leg in a railroad accident. He lugs himself around on that wooden one; like a crank he thinks every day is Sunday and wonders why we do not go to church.

After breakfast I left him to fight with Hatty—my famous half-sister, Harriet Beecher Stowe, the "mother of *Uncle Tom*"—and I beat it to the library. On either side of the chimney are two deep bay-windows; on the north end one large window comes all the way down to the floor, the size of three ordinary windows. I sat in the mid-morning sun and stared at my hands. I could hear the whole family going at each other, pelting each other with words, and I wanted no words at all, I wanted an end to words, I wanted the silence to which all words aspire.

Some wag has opined that there are three kinds of people—Saints, Sinners, and Beechers. Well, from the library I could see Henry in the kitchen, getting a haircut; I watched Henry Ward Beecher sit there while Eunice prowled and snipped about him (she has always cut his hair—though his leonine locks do not take kindly to the shears), and Henry was winking, under his barber sheet, winking at Hatty with that wonderful combination of sentimentality and shrewdness, the sweet and ruthless Big Boy who don't sit still for Mama. Poor Eunice!—the Plymouth faithful call her "The Griffin." Henry is reported to have said, "Her kisses taste of Jeremiah's figs." I hope he didn't say it. But he says, and does, such alarming things: he appears in advertising testimonials, for pianos, for sewing machines, for a—a truss.

Then, when everyone else had retreated upstairs to put the finishing touches on their Sabbath motley, I watched Henry with his nephews and nieces; he led them in Hunt the Keyhole, he was Paymaster at Post Office, and to general delight and shrieks he was Dumb Orator. Henry is not a jowly man, but his big face shakes. I had, simultaneously, the sensation of deepest depression and sublime fun. O murder, the mind goes on, in the library, before church. Especially if one is Beecher. I looked back at my hands and sighed in the sunlight. Outside, two tots were shrilly studious, dismembering an amphibian.

"Tom." The voice startled me, and I fairly jumped, for Eunice was standing there. She waved me back down, and took a chair herself. We sat a moment, quietly, looking at each other, and then she spoke (perhaps Eunice can talk to me only because I am the cold one, "Cold Tom" to the rest of the Beecher dynasty). Eunice laid her words out carefully, like solitaire: "When I got here, Tom, the public began to take my husband away from me. Henry's study wasn't at home anymore, it was at church. And when he went out I used to—" she was silent there in her chair, and I thought to myself, well, she's not going to say it, but then she did: "I used to gasp for breath, and my eyes would fill—it seemed to me as if we had—" the word came up like the four of clubs "—quarreled."

I looked at her, and the word rang in my head because it had no ring at all, no resonance: "quarreled." Her black dress was a panic in her big knuckles. Then her face was suddenly instructed. A yell from Henry upstairs—and she went to attend to him.

I stared at the bookcases where the world's greatest authors held their tongues eloquently. Library? Walhalla! It was here that Matthew Brady made our family sit still, Mary and Catharine flanking Father, to steady his hands for the long exposure. I have the portrait on my desk in Elmira: on the far left Cold Tom is glancing all the way across Charley, Edward, and William to Henry on the far right. There is a look of terror on Tom's face; on Henry's there is a look of—a look of luminous, annoying patience. Oh, sometimes he does annoy me; once Henry invited me to preach in his absence, and when I entered through the side-door and the Plymouth crowd saw me, many of them began to leave, grumbling disappointment. Well, I stood beside the throne at the top of the runway, raised my right hand, and said, "Those who came here to worship Henry Ward Beecher are excused. Those who wish to worship God will remain." It stopped a few. And when the story was relayed to Henry he is supposed to have laughed, "That's Tommy!"

My story becoming his.

And now we go to church: Sabbath Day, Indian Summer of 1859. When I got off that first ferry from

Manhattan this morning, a young Englishman asked me, "How do I find Plymouth Church?" I told him, "Follow the crowd." Indeed, those Sunday ferries are popularly known as "Beecher Boats," and "To Hear Beecher" is as essential a part of a visit to New York as is dinner at Delmonico's. Perhaps I should have said to my Englishman, in his canary-colored waistcoat, "Young foreigner, I will reveal to you this country. Come with me now, and I'll push you into Brother Beecher's Church, accompany you with one of the gentlemen who performs the arduous duty of providing seats for the lucky, and when we are crowded into a pew together, then I shall say to you, "Now, stranger, you have arrived: this is the United States, the New Testament, Plymouth Rock, and the Fourth of July."

Actually, it is Brooklyn Heights, where quiet men in quiet mornings step into their barouches and set out for the ferry. Brooklyn Heights: a fashionable "residential area," the genteel hucksters call it, for the expanding squalor of the urban monster. Brooklyn Heights, a retreat, a wide promontory where those businessmen can escape, to build their fine mansions with lovely lawns and great gardens, where they can raise their families who play croquet on the emerald turf; then, with their thoughts, fathers take that ferry to and from their steaming offices in Manhattan, that hub of business, Wall Street, anonymous, where corners are made to be cut, an impersonal get-ahead world of "snap." Those families in their satined victorias, they are somehow aware of all the swindling, blackmail, all the petty tricks—Ministers of the Gospel lured to brothels by fake calls for missions of mercy (there are twenty thousand prostitutes in New York, and the island is agog over Lola Montez and Ada Clare, the Queen of

Bohemia). If an omnibus pauses to take on a lady we shall have to wait a moment for her skirts to fit through the door. Ah, the Ladies—with their poke bonnets and little velvet tippets; that instant when the skirts are gathered, we catch a glimpse of embroidered stocking. The Gentlemen—well, they are Nicholas Nickleby: frock coats, snug at the waist and flaring out like ballet skirts; skin-tight trousers with huge checks and plaids, held under the boots by straps. Chimney-pot hats on faces surrounded by whiskers.

What, these ladies and gentlemen wonder, happened to the home-town honesty in which they were brought up? In this frightening world of the quick-eye and bluff, what do the mighty teachings of Calvin, and our glorious forefathers, have to say? These people are, in a word, trapped. Between their heritage of a narrow and introspective morality and their intense desire for luxury and respectability. Culture's what they want—Virtue's what they can't give up. They're afraid of foreigners, especially the Catholics, and they feel so decidedly inferior to the great cultures from which the lousy immigrants come. America is bursting at the seams: The West is barbarism; the South, the slave-holding South, is aristocratic arrogance. How can a nation be so on the move and so stranded? It needs a belief! At least a feeling. How can we put all these dreads, confusions, aspirations into words?

That's what Henry's here for. He waits up there on his throne. I sit sweating in the scarlet circle; Hatty on my right; and on her right, our father, Lyman Beecher, "the father of more brains than any man in America." He met us at the door, impatient, muttering about his little house on Willow Street.

And now our Henry walks. Our Henry talks. He gives it to us straight from the shoulder, or straight from the heart, or straight from somewhere between the celestial and the thigh-bone. Parishioners cluttered with gold and jewelry cry, "Help us, Help us."—and Henry does; he is their pater-familias, their fair-haired boy, and their—mother. Henry Ward Beecher, this interloper with a bead on the future, he is no Nicholas Nickleby, he keeps his face clean-shaven, a face all public now, so that it becomes a face noble in aspect, with a brow more broad than high; he carries, and is forever throwing around, his farmer's wide felt hat; his trousers flop loose; he is wearing those Puritan shoes, square-toed, with buckles. A stump speaker who has mistaken his way and stumbled into a church—up there he is not at all a tall man, not quite a portly man, but he is a large man. He is a grand mimic, and now he is "doing" those cowards who took him aside and told him not to ally himself with unpopular causes; all around me I can feel these wealthy Christians come suddenly to attention, riveted in dampness. Henry almost steps on his hat, sidles by it, and bunches himself behind the throne, his eyes glittering with penury of spirit: "IN MY SECOND SERMON AT PLYMOUTH I lifted up the banner and blew the trumpet in the application of Christianity to slavery. But oh, the people said, 'Save your*self,* anyway. What is the use of preaching anti-slavery sermons?' I was tutored. I had friends in high places who whispered in my ear"—Henry, his farmer's frame hunched, cups his hand for hoarse, toady words—"'Prudence; caution; you have opportunity; good society is open to you; do not blight your prospects. There is a chance for you in public life:

do not by rash speaking spoil your opportunity of ascending. Wait!'"

And now, uncurling from that clot of mean-spirited scoundrels, Henry speaks in the full-throat of his own bought-and-paid-for forty-six years: "None of you under thirty can form an adequate conception of the public sentiment during the days of my young manhood. A man that was known to be an Abolitionist had better be known to have the plague. Every door was shut to him. An Abolitionist had the mark of Cain. It was enough to expel a man from Church communion if he insisted on preaching for the liberation of the slaves." Henry strides the tightrope of reciprocal magnetism: "On February 21, 1850, I put the question plainly: 'Shall We Compromise?' Slavery and liberty, one or the other must die. There never was a plainer question for the North. It is her duty openly, firmly, and forever to refuse slavery another inch of territory. It is her duty to refuse her hand or countenance to slavery where it now exists. The Compromise of 1850 is a ball of frozen rattlesnakes; shall we bring them into the house to *thaw*? No, if the compromises of the Constitution include requisitions that violate humanity I will not be bound by them. Not even the Constitution shall make me unjust!"

A ripple of murmuring adoration runs through the moist thirty hundred.

"I REPUDIATE THE OBLIGATION. Never while I have breath will I help any official miscreant in his base errand of recapturing a fellow-man for bondage. May my right hand forget her cunning and may my foot palsy if I ever become so untrue—" Henry's voice, like a tongue of flame, rising, darting, lashing off the great chandelier in the vaulted dome. He is full of moral gunpowder, and there are minor explosions among the Brobdingnagian bouquets on the altar. "If ever I become so untrue to mercy and to religion as not by all the means in my power to give aid and succor to every man whose courageous flight tells me he is worthy of liberty! If in God's providence fugitives ask bread or shelter, raiment or conveyance from us, my own children shall lack bread before they; I will shelter them, conceal them, or speed their flight!"

Sensation! Applause!

In this evangelical greenhouse I turn toward Hatty, rapt as always with that peculiar morbidity of hurt and hungry eyes, dear heart-broken Hatty, ever wounded and seeking the condition of wounds, who has herself had to swallow and now has begun to gulp more than any mortal woman's share of sorrow: her ivory satin dress spreads out just to father's frail black-flannel knees.

"I INVITED FRED DOUGLASS, one day, in those times, to come to Church here. He said, 'I should be glad to, sir, but it would be so offensive to your congregation.' I rode the omnibuses to and from Fulton Ferry, until I saw a sign: 'Colored People Not Allowed.' I instantly got out. I am too much of a Negro to ride in that omnibus."

Father mutters to Hatty, "Henry's a nigar?"

"HOW MANY LEAGUES OFF must a sin be before it is prudent and safe for courageous ministers to preach against it? Let us chastise the courtesans of Paris or the loose virtue of Italy."

Yes, my big brother has got it: he has mined granite, and the Rocky Mountains are his sounding board. A delegation of big money men from the commerical and manufacturing companies came to him for advice about the southern boycott of northern mills; all one long night they sat and talked, and then Henry took pen and scribbled, "MY GOODS ARE FOR SALE, BUT NOT MY PRINCIPLES." It became the rallying cry of the enlightened North, the kind of thing Henry could strike off, in a luxurious room, in the dead of night, among wealthy men.

And he is all on top of us now, a great bear at the lip of the runway, his voice choked with readily available deep emotion, his gray eyes glistening, and he has it, we all know, for his arms go out in a kind of masculine maternity—imploring the Savior—and he cries out, Alone in America with a Conscience Never Clean:

"I AM ASKED TO SPEAK of the duty of the slave to his master. I say that the first duty of every slave who has the power of his own body is—TO RUN AWAY!"

The thunder comes up to him, and he rides on it, positively rides—

"AMERICAN SLAVERY IS NO ANALOGUE or derivative of the Hebrew or any mild form of slavery. It is the extremest and worst form of the Roman slavery; the harshest that the world has ever seen. It is not possible, if God is just, for a nation systematically to violate every natural right of four millions of people and go unpunished. So Sharp's rifles became—Beecher Bibles—"

Henry waits for the applause, and he don't have to wait long. Not in the Church of the Holy Rifles. When he was asked how one can hold a sword in a Christian state of mind, he answered with his own question, "Would you read the Bible to buffaloes?" He took up the collections to send guns to Bleeding Kansas, crates of guns popularly called "Beecher

Bibles." And now he retreats from the throne for a moment, nothing sly about him, as if some message from Congress has been brought in; he's out the little side-door, and we are left buzzing, wondering amongst ourselves. Henry re-appears, in handcuffs, great shackles that he has somehow slipped on himself; he comes down the ramp to show us— Amazement!—he tells us that these are the very chains that held John Brown at Harper's Ferry— Astonishment!—and he holds them out to us. Henry is a statue: he is a work of art. And then in a paroxysm he's got them off, the chains fall with a clangor to the floor, and now Henry is kicking them, kicking them, kicking them, with his buckled Puritan clodhoppers, he is crying, and the fetters are snakes, metal, huge, clanging snakes, he chases them, he kicks and kicks them again, into the threshing floor, stamps them dead, hopping up and down on both feet, and the noise is lost in the massive heartsob of three thousand people crying and cheering and whistling—Henry Ward Beecher kicks John Brown's chains into oblivion, into everlasting Hellfire (into the anteroom) and then comes forward to stand, breathing heavily, covered with perspiration. A cloud of handkerchiefs waves, waves, little flags of Love and Honor and Duty and Self-Sacrifice and the conviction that our lives are not "in vain." We know it will come to War. We know in our bones—War!—yes, our bones know it.

Henry sits upon his throne, re-gathering breath to continue, though I wonder what more can he do? But now his voice is that low sad murmur of lost souls. He is telling us of a young woman, twenty years of age; she is a slave; her owner has informed her, and several cronies in Washington, that if eight-hundred dollars can be raised among the Abolitionists, this owner will accept it and free the young woman. Henry says, "To get her to Plymouth I had to pledge her owner the price or the safe return." He goes through it all, an hysterical spell of terror, sparing little and implying all. A recitation of the horrors of bondage. As Henry roams farther and farther into the recesses of his own heart and our history, the congregation is possessed, possessed:

"Sarah?"

Henry steps once again to the door that leads to the anteroom, and he makes a low bow as if a Lady were there—and one is: she steps out, tall and finely moulded and white as any Lady, dressed in a gown of snow. With her great mass of dark hair wound swarming around her head, more Jewess than Negress, she is a woman rich with a voluptuous Oriental character. Henry extends his hand; she takes it, and they walk—he in black, she in spotless white—a bridal couple down the runway.

Here beside me, Hatty may keel over; she is having a great deal of difficulty, twitching—her head positively twitching. I want to touch her, to calm her, but I see that Father's hand is already there, his gnarled fingers interlocked with her dainty digits. I stare from that up to the runway.

"Sarah?" did Henry say? Venus! We are at an auction block in Charleston. Who bids? Starting at four hundred, gentlemen—four hundred, four hundred—five!—give me six, give me six, gentlemen—I have six—give me six-fifty—going, gentlemen, going—going—

Sarah stares at Henry Ward Beecher. The eyes of the most powerful man in America are all over her—and I, Thomas Kinnicut Beecher, in my head I hand myself a piece of the plan: no, no the slave would not be a man, not a male; no, it could not be one of Hatty's Uncle Toms; no, it would have to be this maiden of infinite grace, this white creature to be dressed in satin finery to sit in the congregation—and standing now above it—FOR SALE—

Oh, it is madness, it is madness—how can one distinguish between Genius and Bad Taste?

"They say that she is one of those praying Methodist niggers."

That is what Henry said.

"She will be sold South—and her owner is, God save us, her—her—" he recites the word like a massive blow to the groin—"her father."

Oh, the Church sees; Plymouth's eyes are open:

"She will be sold down the river—for what purpose you can imagine as you look upon her."

He will not stop, by God he will not.

Yet the minister is a gentleman. A formal whisper: "Take down your hair, my dear."

Tom must leave the House of God. Tom will not bear it, Cold Tom cannot, his hands have departed his wrists, and all he knows is that as Sarah takes down her hair, what else might she take down?, and we contemplate the image of Eve in her earliest garment—in Charleston we shall step up to feel with our fingers her caramel-vanilla flesh, examine her mouth—and the hair comes down in cascades of black silk, raven black hair, hair never to be painted, glossy black, midnight black, such wonderful hair, as it winds and falls and flows on the garment of snow—eight hundred dollars?—we would give our lives for her—and that is what Henry is asking us to do, as voices cry out, shrieks, men and women on their feet, a great bellow of sentiment, heroism and cruelty and blood—Virtue Triumphant, in a panic of sympathy they tear their luxuries from themselves, rip their pockets in reaching for their wallets—buying this light-skinned girl, buying her Methodist *belle-chose*. In the pitch of the frenzy Tom suddenly caves in and cowers down, Tom can feel his body slide out from under his brain and forward into a crouch, and the people are standing in front of Tom picking through memory and intelligence to the little nettle: yes, yes!, Tom cannot see for the salt water running from his brow into his frantic eyes, and Tom's suitcoat must be stained through, for Tom can feel the sweat running under his arms, down his chest: it is no academic question of States' Rights or Constitutional Law; Henry is massing boulders on the little nettle, the question of the human race he has turned up—yes, Slavery is not Man's inhumanity to Man; it is Sexual Depravity. Slavery is not the cruel exploitation of a man forbidden to earn honest money for the honest sweat of his brow; no, slavery is a sin against FAMILY; slavery is adultery, fornication, and concubinage, in comparison with which a Turkish harem is a cradle of virgin purity. HURRAH!

All of which is not lost on mulatto Sarah—her bosom heaving as she stands now amidst the roaring burst of pent-up feeling—released now in bracelets, watches, an explosion of precious gems and diadems, a shower—something obscene is happening all around me and I know again, as I have known from childhood, that I will never get out of it: Henry and his congregation joined in love-making, sobbing to each other—Henry has found himself, found his true love, found Father in all this violence, Beechers are violence, yes, and this is no congregation, no, it is a prosperous mob—Harriet Beecher Stowe, her cheeks streaming, Hatty is up now, and even Father is up, they are worshipping the Wonder of it—

And I cannot find my Family: it is ploughing-ground, it is the threshing floor where bloody grappling is going on, and Cold Tom observes it, resentful, envious, repelled, annoyed, a great pain rising bile-like, a horror put away like pillow-slips—

Pendants and chokers hit the throne; a single voice cannot be heard in this caterwaul of high moral keening, three thousand people vibrating; the world will never end, never end, not when we whore after virtue until we are blinded with adoration—

Henry so ineluctably there: "I WILL MAKE THY WINDOWS AGATES!" Henry Ward Beecher all over us: "YOU ARE CRYSTALLINE, YOUR FACES ARE RADIANT!" And then the last push, Henry plunging to the hilt, Henry's cry transfiguring Heaven:

"YE ARE GODS!"

Fifteen years ago, when Cold Tom was fresh out of Illinois College, he didn't know where to go. Father was determined that all seven of his boys would be preachers of the Gospel. I wrote to him:

Father, the profession which you practice with such happiness to yourself and all your hearers—it is impossible for me to enter it with so many doubts. I fear this announcement gives you pain, perhaps causes you much sorrow while reading it. But I have been on a short allowance of spiritual grog for some time. How can I man a life boat wherein I can cruise for shipwrecked sinners? Especially when I will have to bail hard, caulk cracks, and scull hard with only half an oar left, to escape Davy Jones's locker myself?

Well, Father came right down. He sat with me all one afternoon, ravenously ate his supper, and listened to me project alternate careers. Engineering, I said. Law, I said, Medicine. Oh, Father, a clock and watchmaker, but not a minister of the Gospel. I told him, as he pushed back and sat there with a bit of biscuit on his chin, that today's Christian is but a man standing in the rain to admire and praise his noble house.

Father stood up, came round the table, and put his hand on my shoulder; in a whisper he said, "Tom, do you not know that you cannot love, and be examining your love at the same time?"

I turned and looked up at him. I was shaking.

Then he was Lyman Beecher: "Tom, some people, instead of getting evidence by running at life, take a dark lantern and get down on their knees"—he did so—"and crawl on the boundary up and down to make sure they have crossed over"—and there was Lyman Beecher, crawling on my bare floor, away from my chair, across to the sideboard, coming around the other side of the table—and then he was up: "If you want to make sure, Tom, *run!* When you see the celestial city, my son, when you hear the songs of the angels, you'll know you're across."

"But Father—"

On the morrow he had decided what to do. He was going to send me to Henry, out in Indiana. There lay salvation: Tom would be Henry Ward's lay assistant; perspicacious antagonists, the elder brother would bring round the morbid reprobate. I said, "Well, I suppose I could go and help Henry . . . if . . ."

"*Tom,*" Father said, "You must go to Heaven,

you must not go to Hell, and you must not continue Stupid!"

Dearest Father.

So I went. A family conspiracy. I had already learned from Henry, years before, what Father's absolute insistence on "conversion" could be—or at least I had seen something of what it could be, what a frightened child could know of it. When Henry was nineteen, just on the edge of his famous "conversion," I was eight. I followed him late one afternoon as he was taking out a great bucket of slops, and I saw him in the sunset—the sky a great bank of thunderheads, not pink, not rose or scarlet, but orange: Heaven was a popular dream, clamor and state. Henry lifted the slop bucket and threw out its mighty swill, rocked back on his heels, glanced skyward and caught his breath. I wanted to see what my big brother was looking at, and then I did see it: a bird—too black to be a swallow and too small for a crow, it was heading off away from the sun, all across orange, a lonely little strongheart against the sky drama: The bird was so sharply strong, so inexpressibly clear—I turned back to Henry with the slop bucket, and he was weeping.

Now, an eight-year-old worries. Henry was like a God to me—no, he was just so plain and tender and good to me as a child; no, he was the best to me, the best of all: Henry at nineteen bawling out his life in a slop bucket, I remember it terribly, just the sight of it, and years later I came to realize that he is—he is helpless in beauty!—the bird in the sky was no talisman of any local pain (I had experienced the uncontrollable weeping of an older schoolboy, weeping when his cart slid on the ice and ran over a rabbit, and I sat beside that boy and patted his hand,

and I knew he wasn't weeping for the bunny, he was weeping for his younger brother who had just been consigned to the frozen turf)—no, young Henry was weeping only and completely for the sunset and the bird, all by themselves, alone together, meaningless.

And, on the way to Indiana to get converted, it was bothersome that I had Henry's moment confused in my mind with Father's great statement of *his* conversion. Bothersome that I saw Henry's as merely secular, a vulgar version of Father's. For once Lyman Beecher was alone with a great sky shattered by Aurora Borealis, from horizon to zenith, a blood-red arch. Father wrote, "I knew what fire was, and what forever was." Henry could not say it so finely. Beecher boys don't live up to Father. It would not be Henry's luck, or lot, or precinct, to have an Aurora Borealis; he would have a soft orange and a little dark bird.

We decline. So we decline. Who mortgages Heaven?

And when I arrived in Indiana, Henry did not bother me with credal logic; he said, "If you wish to compute your doctrinal latitude you may discover much more than you wish to know, Tommy. Evade exact definition, and keep the fruits of faith."

I muttered something about preserving them in rigid self-inquiry. But Henry had breathed too much moral oxygen to tolerate my *tic doulourex;* he took me in his arms and said, "Know how much deeper *feeling* is than *thinking!*" And then he had me. There were no arguments. Nothing was proved.

Q: Can you tell how the bones of the unborn babe grow in the womb?

A: So Christ was formed in Consciousness. Like some black bird high-flying across an orange thunderhead, then drops down through smoke into a walled city fortified against all comers, carrying under its wing a message of rescue.

So my life—my life—clattered along yet a little longer, like a cart with a sprung axle (I spent two years with Father, and removed for another two as Principal of the Hartford High School), and then—then—received my calling. In Elmira, New York. Where I was free to expound my discourses on Negative Preference—none of Henry's runaway-horse evangelism. Father sent on to me a letter from one of his old pupils at Lane Seminary who had attended my Sabbath service:

Your son's voice is very fine, clear as a trumpet, and his articulation uncommon. The sermon was a very strange and eccentric one, full of strange and sometimes undignified passages, but it was full of feeling, not well balanced exactly but real. This Thomas is full of sensibility and will make a noble preacher—if he does not run wild entirely.

Yes. Thank you, Father.

But my congregation sustains me. Indeed, I am quite popular among the townspeople—and very un-popular with some other local ministers. A certain Methodist Divine was quoted in the press: "The reputation of the entire Beecher family for eccentricity is rank, but 'Tom' Beecher is the worst of the lot." Well I am. I keep my office in a dilapidated tenement house downtown; I drink beer. I put repentant prostitutes into the homes of my parishioners (the McCulloughs have put "Sally" into their will and testament, and "Irene" has convinced the Williams boy that she's "done with backslidin'!"). My battered old cap and threadbare jacket become increasingly remarkable. But the grandest legend about me is my—my—

Tricycle! I made it, over a period of months, with the help of a blacksmith and a coachman: It is man-size, a shining beauty of pine and leather and rosewood and iron, a phaeton self-propelled, I can sail down Water Street—I say that the third wheel is for stability on the ice, but it ain't, it's for stability after the beer. Three wheels: faith, hope, and longevity.

Henry says, "I always get the blues when I go toward Elmira." But I have become enamored of "upstate"—the way the citizens band together in our annual emergencies, when snowstorm turns into blizzard, where life stops and death is at hand. Once I was on the way to preach the funeral of a stately patriarch whose Easter-Extra allowed me to go ahead and build my chariot from my diagrams, I was on the way—when a man with his cart overturned in a snowy ditch needed some help. I was in a hurry, pedalling past, and the man uttered an oath about that "Goddamned tricycle!" and I pulled into a long slow skid, diligently pedalled back to him, and said, "Begging your pardon, brother, I am about to put into the ground the body of the man who paid for this Goddamned tricycle, and his widow is weeping"— the man was so astonished to see a minister of the Gospel speak his language that, come summer, we painted both our houses together. Robert Lester Martin and Thomas Kinnicut Beecher; Bob and I talked together, worked together, he was a real

Kentucky chiaroscuro, with half-a-hand missing, and he wanted to be Chief of Police. His talk was obscene, his behavior strict and kind—which got him elected. He deals with trouble, and so do I. The young women in my congregation bring me their loneliness, their Elmira loneliness. A man from the country wishes my name on his circular for a school. A woman in failing health by confinement to sewing does not know what to do; behind in her books, she does not wish charity. A man calls to inquire after a friend he has lost sight of; over coffee he admits to a quarrel, his fault. A kind woman calls in behalf of a boarder who is out of place, desponding, will throw himself away. An honest-looking man comes next, is out of work, has heard from "Constable Bob" that "your riverince" is a kind man. Another wants to get his family out from Ireland; can pay half, if someone will intercede with shipowners to trust him the balance. An old lady alcoholic desires conversation. A stranger has died. I look at my hands, catch my cap, and mount my tricycle!

But now the unspeakable horror was upon us. War. A "Civil" War. No Revolution, for the loser cannot go home. And Brother Henry was harassing Lincoln, proclaiming "the extraordinary want of executive administrative talent at the head of the government." Henry would not settle for less than articles of emancipation. I wrote to him,

I think you are in error, and doing great harm by a most noble overestimate of men and public sentiment. I am satisfied that the day you succeed in writing your magnificent principles on our national banner you will have only a flag and a sentiment; the army, the men, with one consent will say, "We ain't going to fight for the niggers." I can answer for rural New York. (Can answer for Illinois and Indiana, too.) The more emancipation you talk, the less recruits you can enlist.

His answer was all perfunctory, for he was after Lincoln (who himself had worshipped in Plymouth Church whatever Honest Abe worships). At a time when the average Congregational Church in America had a membership of eighty, Henry Ward Beecher was holding forth to a church of three thousand; in his "Star Papers," his books, in the *Independent,* he was reaching hundreds of thousands. He had the power of a dictator, and he was using it. Lincoln wrote him a bitter letter, asking him, "Is thy servant a dog?" A legend began: in the darkest days of the war Lincoln took a night train to Brooklyn to talk with Henry. The legend must at least have had some foundation in fact; when an impertinent young reporter for a Washington paper asked his President, the Commander-in-Chief, "Who is *the* American of our time?" Honest Abe made one of his characteristic pauses, and responded, "Beecher."

January 1, 1863: Henry got what he wanted. Emancipation. And he was exhausted. He was ill. Plymouth raised money to send him to Europe for recovery, a rest and a vacation. I found it curious, then, as I still do, that perhaps his greatest triumph in public began because he was exhausted in public. He said that he would make no speeches in England. Several British organizations urged him to command their platforms; but "no," he said, "we shall not, bye and bye, care a pin whether the English think well or ill. How glad I would be if I need not speak. In truth, I have no heart for it." It seemed as if he could escape into silence. He kept quiet for weeks; he quietly crossed the Channel and rested in France and Italy. I wrote to him, "Your silence in England is golden. It satisfies all your family and your friends here at home. Everybody, without exception, thinks you have managed sensibly and wisely."

But did America think they had merely sent Henry Ward Beecher to London to see the Queen? In '63? The England of the Trent Affair? The Emerald Isle's textile factories and cotton mills closed, and Britain beginning to lean dangerously toward the Confederate cause? Henry had been so dazzled on his first trip, in 1850, so innocently plunged into sudden melancholy, that he cried out, "What if I should die abroad?" He had been contemplating, unabridged, the Beauty of Time, Henry who had always been impervious to the records of history (he called a library "the soul's burial ground—the Bodleian is a Dead Sea of books"). The Temperance Man had gurgled, "I am here to be intoxicated!"— but now it was War, now he was on that kindred foreign soil. To rest himself, or to be a valiant warrior? The Liverpool *Courier* announced, "Mr. Beecher's views on slavery are too violent and unreasonable to meet with much favour from thoughtful people." He said he would speak! It was his duty! And he was met by armed mobs (his sponsors had thoughtfully armed themselves as well). Henry was led, an unsuspecting lamb, into halls brimming with boiling cauldrons of Bulldog humanity. What terror my big brother must have felt. Henry still had not overcome his stage fright; indeed, he would never get over it. A veteran of twenty years of public address, he still could say, after a successful performance, "So the agony is over, and I am safely through another dreaded job. But then, I shall dread the next one just as much. Success never inspires confidence; the next time's just as bad." How he must have longed for the safety of Plymouth, a few hours with his color-opiates could get a sermon writ. (And he had always been such a bad sailor, he spent the voyage from Naples to Liverpool in his cabin, coughing up food he never ate.) The coach led him through the streets where riots were in progress, the British public clamoring and wailing. Our poor sailor said, "I am on board ship, addressing through a speaking-trumpet a tornado on the sea and a mutiny among the men, the whole world's oceans under my feet." Weary, sick, lost—Henry Ward Beecher looked out at the thousand-headed monster; it laughed, it laughed a thousand laughs at him. So what did Henry do, what could he do?

Laugh back. He fell into a barbaric joke: "You are a colossal brute. Look about you. Am I wrong? Are you not a colossal brute? Which do you prefer—a lust for triumph or a sense of equilibrium?"

The first. Great placards warned of his pernicious intent:

MEN OF MANCHESTER—WHAT RECEPTION CAN YOU GIVE THIS WRETCH, SAVE UNMITIGATED DISGUST AND CONTEMPT? HIS IMPUDENCE IN COMING HERE IS ONLY EQUALLED BY HIS CRUELTY AND IMPIETY!

And he was introduced as the Reverend Mr. Henry Beecher Stowe.

But he stood strong against the gathered scorn and rage, somehow stood there, in his Puritan buckled shoes, waiting out the shouts, pausing, trying to speak, waiting again, then shouting back at them, then beginning to be most gracious in address: "Oh, in England you have but three hundred miles in diameter one way and eight hundred the other. We Americans have got a whole continent to take care of." Why, they shouted, don't you go back and take care of it? Henry smiled. "You English are five hours ahead of us every day, and we have to work with all our might to make up those five hours." O, Merry England: "Never were mother and daughter set forth to do so queenly a thing in the kingdom of God's glory as England and America. The same blood is in us. We have the same mission amongst the nations of the earth. The day is coming when the foundations of the earth will be lifted out of their places and there are two nations that ought to be found shoulder to shoulder and hand in hand for the sake of Christianity, and these nations are Great Britain and America. Together—for religion and liberty—we will be a match for the world." The Great War in America was being "kindled not by the young but by the old and sage as well." The northern Army was being "fed not by the ignorant and violent but by scholars, women, Christians. Our recruiting ground is chiefly among academies and colleges, in Sabbath schools—the Union Army is an Evangelical Host. Not acting from desires of conquest but with an enthusiasm for an abstract sentiment, an invisible quality—love for law, liberty, Christ!"

And he won. Henry won the way Henry always wins: by bribery, flattery, invocation, piety, but mainly by the sheer, brute, glorious fact of his presence, the battering ram of his soul and the tower of his immovable person—he won by being

Beecher—up there on the platforms of Liverpool, Manchester, Glasgow, and London—those English speeches becoming all one great speech, on Free Labor, Moral Right, Practical Expediency, Good Morals turning into Good Business—laughing at the limeys, scoffing at their pistols, weeping at the wretched plight of the slaves, stamping his foot on expediency (while pocketing profit), releasing the host of American moral passion in oratorical splendour. Gorgeous Henry!

America greeted his return, the conquering hero, the one and only man who could turn English sentiment around, the man who averted English intervention on the side of the South (although—although the English just may have read a few words in their newspapers about the fall of Vicksburg—may have noticed a column or two about the repulse of the Rebs at Gettysburg). But Henry Ward Beecher was now, as Dr. Holmes called him, "Our Minister Plenipotentiary." He was our Liberator—he who had sent Sharp's Rifles to Bleeding Kansas, he who had issued the finest antislavery manifestoes and turned the auction block into the pillory of conscience, he who was settling America's quarrel with Calvinism, he who was the emerging champion on Woman's Rights—in short, the most popular man in all America. Now he could say it—he could say what he had so often said that every man dreams of saying—"My dearest Mother, I am a hero!"

Mother, always Mother. He had proclaimed, "I have more communion with my mother, whom I never saw except as a child three years old, than any living being." As for his step-mother, my mother, he scoffed: "It would have been easier for me to lay my hand on the block and have it struck off than to open my thoughts to her." Harriet said that when their own dear mother, their lovely Roxana, died, "We were told that she had been laid in the ground, and we were told she had gone to Heaven. Whereupon Henry, putting two things together, resolved to dig through the ground and go to find her; for being discovered under Catherine's window one morning digging with great zeal and earnestness, she called him to know what he was doing, and lifting his curly head, with great simplicity he answered, 'Why, I am going to heaven to find Ma.'"

And now, now upon his return from England, he had found her. My dearest Mother, I am a hero.

But no sooner had he found his mother than we all lost Father. He died in '63. Lyman Beecher, standing up in my mind—his white hair floating behind him, Father besplashed and besplattered on his smoking steed, his saddlebags crusted with mud and ice—he departed on his chariot of fire. Father, who himself had preached against slavery, in England, nearly twenty years before, at the first World's Temperance Convention in London. And my soul swept back to those two years between Indiana and Hartford, when Father and I lived together in isolation, when no one else in the family would have him; Father and I spent long mornings walking in the woods, trading stories and little jokes, gruff endearments, forever poking fun at each other. It was related to us, during that time, that Henry Ward Beecher had no policy on baptism—that he baptized by sprinkling, affusion, or immersion; any way, damp or soaking, to Christ. Father remembered the old southern farmer who was asked if he believed in infant baptism, and replied, "*Believe* in it? Man, I've seen it *done*." And one night—oh, we had heard about all the literary men who paid homage to Henry Ward Beecher, like Mr. Henry David Thoreau, who pronounced him "a magnificent pagan," and Mr. Whittier, who said, "that throbbing heart is what I mean in my poetry." But Father was worried about another poet, who had sprouted his *Leaves of Grass* right down the street in Brooklyn. Henry called upon Walt, and they visited Fowler and Wells' Phrenological Depot, roamed galleries, the waterfront, made friends with the hack drivers, probably "diffused their flesh in lacey jags"—Father worried about that; he said, "My Henry Ward ought steer clear of the barbarian." But Father decided to test the waters, to loaf and invite his soul in the famous *Leaves of Grass,* and one night I heard him in the kitchen howling with laughter; I poked my head in, and he handed me Mr. Whitman's shocking appeal to the Body Electric; poor Mr. Whitman misspoke himself in his great importuning of the dynamo-lady; he promised to pour his "Semitic fluid" into her—oh, how Father laughed until the tears came. *Semitic fluid!*

I was seeing a young lady then, who was an Episcopalean, and I wanted her to stay Episcopalean, but Father was restless and out of sorts. Then suddenly he came round: "Go to the Episcopal Church, Tom, your mother loved it"—and my soul sank, my father cannot give me even that comfort!—my mother didn't love the Episcopal Church, no, Father, it was your first wife, Roxana Foote, not Harriet Porter, Father, my mother didn't—and then I swallowed all my imprecations and chill, for he said, "Tom, I love you; you mustn't go 'way and leave me. I want one chicken under my wing." So I stayed, one little chicken with the old rooster.

And now—he's dead.

I pedalled my tricycle across the crystal mud, down to the depot. I boarded my car, and went to Brooklyn for the funeral. Gazing out the frosted window at the snowbelt, the Chemung Valley, I remembered how Father was never cold, never cold. After a blizzard had piled its white fury against the house, Father would cut a twenty-foot tunnel outward from the kitchen door, carrying the snow through the house in a barrel, us brats crying with the cold and slapping our hands and stamping our feet, Father working like a dynamo, sweating, sweating. After the job was done he would bring out his violin and take off his shoes for a barn jig, the old "double shuffle."

On the groaning train to the City I saw it, I saw it and drifted into sleep: Life and Death began to ring in one music, the screeching of the cars, fumes and slow rocking and sudden stops; the funeral I was going to became the funeral I have never quite left—this world is a dream, a dark-colored, chiming, old family house. Years ago—when I "proposed"—it was in her parlor, after a funny tea, a dull and rainy afternoon, Olivia Day's face was suddenly lighted in unshed tears, and Thomas Kinnicut Beecher stood there tongue-tied, saying to himself that Livy's face was "the human face," now and forever, as in the great paintings, but old masters don't breathe and Liv's face was such a wonderful face: she loved me, that's what her face meant, it meant that she knew, and it was that way for her too, seeing whatever my poor dumb face was up to, and her brimming eyes spelled out heartache, spelled out life as a tragic understanding and a shy belief. We fell in love, we saw ourselves doing it, laughed, and then kept on doing it blind. And we got ourselves married. And all at once she was with child, and—and we hold each other, by the Ever-living God we hold each other—and she and the baby—a boy—she died borning our son. Liv died, our son never quite lived—and I buried them. Ever since, I have been, somehow, somehow lost; a Blue Spruce about twenty feet high stands just beyond their graves—

The train lurched, and I was awake. I sneezed, and blew my nose. Father despised and feared the passivity of mere "Suffering"—his motto was, "Agonize, *Agonize!*" I blew my nose again, and muttered into the rag, Such a comfort!

Cold Tom. The family says that Tom don't feel much; don't Tom seem cold—about Livy's death—sometimes don't he seem cold toward us?—

O Great God, my God—cold?

So I'm cold. And at the house on Columbia Heights, Tom did not behave properly, Tom who is—correctly—regarded as "Father's favorite." Tom could not turn on his faucets for the gathered family. First Catharine took him aside. She said, "I feel myself repulsed by your outward manner and style of language." I looked at my boots. Oh, Caty! I was thinking of years past, those months when I had her—Catharine—on my hands, after Father persuaded me to accompany her on her speaking tour. I was thinking of the time when I read her incredible speeches from the platforms (after all, I told myself then, if Calvin Stowe can read Harriet's speeches. . .),but Catharine was proclaiming *Truth Stranger than Fiction,* her daring adventure to indict the clergy by charging it with the destruction of women. I sat in those insufferable railway cars with her, she was abject from hysteria and fits of paralysis; I lay awake and listened to her moans through the walls of dingy hotels. Then we visited dear old brother Charley, and he said to me in his barn, the toe of his boot bothering manure, "Now I know Caty has peculiarities that repel some from her. And yet it seems sad to me to see her cast out from the family circle by Mary, and Hatty, and Henry." Charley, kicking at a chicken: "Cannot Catharine be made to feel more of the warm family sympathy in her loneliness?" So I got back into an iced and groaning car—Catharine's forehead glistening with pain; Charley waving from the station, chasing his hat down the sleet of the platform.

And now I sat in Henry's parlor, with all the railway cars, all the funerals trawling my brain, listening to Catharine call me Cold. Upstairs in the nursery there were sounds of children and grandchildren and great-grandchildren—and my brain blurted out to me like noise, not thought: where's my Olivia? I need her at my arm, and our boy should be up there—I need, I need—

Henry. He came in to rescue me from Catharine; he came in ready to preach the funerary oration, for he had been careful, before he left for England, to write one out; he had read it to our father for his approval and corrections, but when Father had raised his frail head and asked, "Is there not too much encomium?" Henry had said simply, "Hush, Father, you are dead."

And now he was. His life rapid, terrible, and glorious.

Eunice took me aside. Eunice, uncompromising woman, who allies her life with Henry's—Henry who has a genius to be loved, who is Public Property. And often mistaken, for he so suffers, so hungers for affection. They are the most mismatched people, and a perfectly married pair—Eunice is Eunice, no nonsense about her; and Henry is Henry, delighting in nonsense. Her tears are in an underground well; his on a giant tureen. His boisterous gaiety and horseplay hurt her, hurt her in the sternness of her spine. His parishioners enjoy him, the way he ladles out emotion to them as if restoring a birthright: "Here now, I know you dasn't, but do notice how nourishing it is anyway"—and since they are straight-laced, not rock-ribbed, they go toddling off with his eggnog.

Now Eunice wanted to talk to me privately. We are here to observe the death of Father—our gathering plunges her into the deaths of her children. In 1840 she gave birth to a dead son. After three weeks of false labor. And, later, when her little George Lyman died, such a pretty child, and they buried him in an Indiana snowstorm, she wrote to me: "Oh, Tom, dear Georgie! I have the wildest longing to *look into his grave and see.* . . ." When they arrived in Brooklyn, their one-year-old, Catharine, died. In 1850 Eunice gave birth to twin boys, who didn't live six months. Four children still living—but five have died, and she is worn out giving birth to the dead and the soon dead. Meanwhile her husband is the toast of the country, a man who says, "My wife is jealous of my work, and my children think that July and August are the only months in which they have a father."

Now Eunice said to me, "Some years back, Tom, you wrote Henry a letter—and, of course, we save all the letters."

She handed it to me. "A letter about Georgie—about our little Georgie's death."

And now I read my own words:

The highest conception of Christian heroism is Christian motherhood—and motherhood must also be a foul incongruity. To me, Eunice's pain must be the greatest thing. The death of your little boy chimes in with a unison of evil. I say it was bad. It was wrong. It is of the devil, who is the devil because he has the power of death. I hate him, hate his works in a world where Jesus could not live, my Livy could not live, nor your boy. Some people may live too long—but everybody dies too soon. Enthusiasm is a good thing to 'em who has any. But I have shaken the stoutest arguments upon which men build their conceit of truth and they all rattle with weakness.

Well, there's a Christian minister for you. I looked at the date—yes, that would have been written when I was living with Father. Those words peeping out, crowing out from under his wing. Why does Eunice, now . . . ?—I looked up at her, and she was waiting for me.

"Henry and my brother," she said, "were discussing the marriage of a classmate—we were all so young then, none of us yet twenty, having 'lots of fun,' as the children say." Eunice stood there, surrounded by death, famished for light and life. "Henry asked my brother, 'Who would want to marry a girl who can't sing?' I thought Henry meant me. I ran out of the room in tears." Eunice Bullard Beecher—"I cried, and I ran from Papa's parlor, and—Henry, in a rush of remorse, Henry fell in love with me."

I looked up at Eunice, the pain of pain survived—and I remembered a scrap of a story I'd heard, that when she was nineteen her father threw hot soup at her because her dress was cut too low in the bodice. Eunice Bullard, about to have her life torn away from her, all unknowing, about to become a—*Beecher*—and now I said to her, "Ah, but Henry does so love you."

"Ah," she turned to me her terrible small smile, "but I can't sing."

Hatty called from the kitchen, and Eunice went in. Hatty thinks *she* should advise Henry, and the two women continually fight for their rights. Hatty once wrote to Eunice, "I thought you were such a good-for-nothing saucy baggage, and yet I cannot help loving you, sins, sinner, and all." Eunice made the mistake of showing the letter to Henry; a grave mistake—for he took pleasure in displaying the epistle! And now Catharine joining the fray, using on Eunice what she once used on me—Caty says an unmarried lady cannot stay by herself in a hotel, and so she visits them for months on end. I could hear her in the kitchen, "Now, Eunice, I fancy I shall have to listen to some of your speeches about not caring to speak with you—my not loving you—liking you only because you are Henry's wife and all that trumpery!"

Can't sing? Cold Tom sneaked out of the house, down the street, and dived into a saloon. I was overwhelmed with angry sadness. I wisely fell in love with the painted lady in the swan-boat hanging in supercilious velvet over the bottles.

The hour came round when we had to endure the throng at Plymouth, Lyman Beecher's State Funeral. I sat with all my brothers and sisters, looked up, and thought, Henry is the best—if I was Father's favorite, then Henry is the most like Father; for versatility of talent and for warmth of affection and happiness he is hardly second to

Father. Henry threw away that prepared text and spoke of Father's days at Lane Seminary, Father standing before his forty students, Father contemplating the great dusk that preceded Creation. Eternal glory and inevitable ruin await, if God decides that creation will go forward. Father played God, and asked, "Shall I *create?*—or *not?*" And the forty students harrahed the harvest of the soul: "Create! *Create!*"

Henry Ward Beecher strode toward us with the divine memory of Father: "He was a hero! He carried the revival torch across the prairies on his long-boned and fast-walking sorrel, with those well-worn and ill-fitting saddlebags—as courageous as Paul, as gentle as John. I remember the Sunday of my ordination, in the White Water Valley. Father got there Saturday night. When he had arrived on Friday night at the termination of the Canal, he had sixty-nine miles to ride, the road terrible—it was impossible to do it on Saturday—so waiting for the moon to rise he started at ten o'clock on Friday night"—Henry stood before us on the runway, giving us the glad tidings, his eyes misted with memory and love, his voice exuberant—"I was but twenty-nine and Father just seventy. He rode all the night and all day Saturday, and preached at my ordination, then preached again that night, as hearty as a buck. I remember—I remember my first sight of him, Saturday, when he got off his steaming horse, and after a rubdown he ventured out and bagged game with a rifle, to repay the hospitality."

It was just right for us, and too much for Henry; he began to weep, stood there weeping, this magnificent warrior who had conquered England and now had lost his father; Henry fell back into his great chair. At last he murmured, his voice so soft, so spent with War, so sick with War: "When I was a little boy I went into my father's room, and he put his hand upon my head, and with tones of great kindness and love he said, 'You have got the toothache, my dear boy. Come get in with me and cuddle down by my side'—and how that filled me with affection, and such gladness that I forgot the toothache. It was lost. And I slept."

The family sat around Henry's house for two days, receiving the crowds who came to pay homage to Lyman Beecher. Cold Tom was given the assignment of writing a letter to Brother Jamesy, the littlest Beecher of us all, now in China, preaching the Gospel to sailors. I was to tell him of Father's death, and all I could think was that now Father could bedevil Jamesy no longer. Handsome, pampered, violent Jamesy, who has been in trouble all his life, from earliest boyhood, who has threatened suicide time and time again until the family pays him only habitual annoyance and mediocre dread. Sitting in the upstairs study I wrote to James, felt woe toward our Carolina Hotspur, with his Bowie knife, so winsome and pretty and surly. I took two hours to write him "Father died"—for I remembered Jamesy saying to me once, "If Agony will help, let me know, and I'll 'Agonize, *Agonize.*'" I thought at the time that he was right: you do not rescue the drowning man by going down with him. I sat there under the steady hiss of the lamp, my pen poised over the paper, thinking of when I had been closest to Jamesy. It was when I took the principalship at the Hartford High School—only to discover that nine out of ten pupils were of no home feeling, who gloried in cheating me, and took more pleasure in seeing me whip a fellow than they would in seeing me labor for his welfare. Edward had said it was my duty to cane them. And that was when word came in that our baby brother Jamesy had assaulted a fellow student at Dartmouth—in Chapel!—and Jamesy came to me in Hartford to complain about the terrors of ambitious insignificance—I, Thomas Kinnicut Beecher, who keep every meagre record of that high court—and Jamesy took my money, and then we suddenly discovered that we were, indeed, brothers, full brothers, Jamesy and I, and that we felt toward each other—oh, we felt bitterness, and we felt tenderness. Both those. Which for some reason made me stop whipping the boys at the Hartford High School. (And then it was worse: the boys began to worship me; my delinquents turned into my darlings.) Jamesy went off to visit Isabella, and upon his return, Jamesy opined to me, his face close and full of drink, "I am sure there runs a streak of insanity in our mother's three children—I recognize it in you and myself. Belle is absolutely unconscious and is therefore the craziest of the three."

"If she gets well," I said to him, "she can't do much good, and if she grows worse, she cannot do much harm."

Jamesy sighed. "The years will clear us out, all three of us, and in a dozen years or so if anybody should ask who were those Beechers, there will be nobody able to answer the question."

We laughed—all bitterness, all tenderness.

So Jamesy got me and Henry together with him, to advise him about his life. Henry looked upon Jamesy and began, "Know how much deeper *feeling* is than *thinking*—" and Cold Tom recoiled, recoiled in hurt, hurt that deepened into horror, and then I just watched my big brother administer the extract to my little brother, and I thought it was absolutely terrible—and absolutely necessary. So Jamesy went to China, a missionary. And now, in Henry's upstairs study, I ended my letter to Jamesy. I could not think of a thing to say, I could not quite say anything. So I concluded my short note with something I thought he would enjoy:

> The wisdom of the serpent is not incompatible with the harmlessness of the dove.

Cold Tom. I suppose my view of life *is* dark—such a small hope for felicity, such infinite possibilities for suffering. But Jamesy and I, the boys of "the second Beecher brood," we have seen radiance in that darkness, and do not descant by the hour on that which engenders strife and yields no profit. So I sealed the letter, put out the lamp, and went downstairs, out onto the porch, and watched Edward pick at his wooden leg. I hated him. For reasoning me to death. I remembered how once I almost worshipped him, but am undeceived now; either Edward is insane or else not a Christian. If religion were to make me another Edward, I say God deliver me.

Then our beautiful Isabella, with splotches of blood and nerves in her face, was upon me, entreating me to marry again. Ten years ago, when Livy and I were carefully planning, Belle upbraided me for stalling: "You rather desire to prolong your courtship than to abridge it, Tom—perfectly content with your bird in the bush." And I said, "I am far more disposed to hear her warble from the spray than to hear her sing from a cage." Which made Belle storm out of the room ten years ago, as now she storms off the porch. Cold Tom, the mute witness to tumult and tragedy, a man whose life is proxy and anecdote. But who are we?—all of us on our wild courses, weighing anchor in claptrap and finding snug harbor in heroic discipleship. That Beecher Boat from Manhattan to Brooklyn Heights—we are all Beecher boats, and now Catharine is in the Arctic Ocean, and Edward is on a tramp steamer from Liverpool to New York, regular and flatulent, and Jamesy is quite literally in the China Sea, and Isabella is in her Canarys, and I'm in Tierra del Fuego, and Henry—well, Henry has always been in Hawaii.

I watched him. With my bags packed for my return to Elmira on the night train, I watched Henry: he remained, even in grief, an incurable flirt. I said to him in my heart: Be careful, brother mine, be careful! One might as well argue Bishop Berkeley with an Anthropographus. It was Harriet who started the sentimental rumor that Henry Ward Beecher never had a toy. Balderdash! We all had toys, we *made* them—Catharine's Old Testament dolls, the Queen of Sheba with her chariot fashioned from a scooped-out pumpkin, a nigger driver with four crook-neck squashes for horses. I remember all the games, "Telling Scott"—when Father would rush in after supper and say, "Come now, who can get the most out of *Ivanhoe?*" Hilarious evenings, boisterous sessions, ending with a hymn and Father's tender prayer. Our household was magic, magic!

And in the mental wandering of his final years, Father summoned us all, to be his audience to his life. After *Uncle Tom* had become a sacred text, after Henry had become our National Chaplain. Father told us, day after day, his autobiography. Charley was writing it down that week I was there in '62. Father said, "Curious, this thing of personal identity. Here I am now, an old man telling you a story about a little boy. And yet I feel that I am the same person now that I was then." He fell into silence. We looked at each other. "Once at the saw-mill," he said, biting on his lip for a kernel of corn, that characteristic gesture, his choppers going after a little piece of food not yet 'et, "I hooked a pickerel without bait—how I whopped him out!" Silence. Edward's sigh, as if it were, somehow, embarrassing. And the silence unravelled, the final gauze bandaging and mummification, the veins on the back of his palsied hands—and all at once Father in his heresy trial at Lane: "Mr. Wilson made me think of a partridge on a dead limb, watching me when I am trying to get a shot at him." Catharine was waiting it out, her eyes downcast—she will never forgive Father, and never escape him. Henry leaning forward to behold—Henry, a paradigm of innocence! Acceptable only if one has great talent. Eunice shelling peas—and baying sepulchral, without a sound.

At the very end of his life, trapped and exiled in that close apartment on Willow Street, Father could still jump a five-barred fence. But mostly he would sit, quietly, for hours, at the window. He had a third wife, but he was slipping letters to Roxana in the Hereafter. Observing him on his deathbed a granddaughter said, "Must have been handsome in his youth!" The old man opened one eye and said, "Am still!"

His last words were, "Part of me, part of *me*."

Back in Elmira I could not listen to the silence of Father not being in the world. I took out his fiddle—for he had left it to me—and I stared at it, held it. I dreamt of him too often. And I worried about Henry. When I read of the theatre people sawing a lady in half at Barnum's Museum I thought of Henry selling "Sarah" to the Plymouth congregation. Henry and P.T., I heard, were friends who watched each other carefully.

Then the War was over, and Lincoln was dead—and as we grieved, I thought again: "Mother—Mother—" for Honest Abe had been a curious kind of Motherly Father to us, in his quiet female sadness, wearing his lady shawl. Mother—Mother—

And the granite of Henry's influence began to

erode. He was preaching conciliation to the South. The North cried for the execution of Jeff Davis, and Henry preached against the confiscation of Reb property; immediately upon the surrender of Richmond he called for a general amnesty: "The Abolition of Slavery is not a punishment but a blessing." When Robert E. Lee was being hounded out of the presidency of Washington College in Virginia, Henry said, "The War ceased, and he laid down his arms—who could have been more modest, more manly, more true to his own word and honor?" In short, "I think it to be the great need of this nation to save the self-respect of the South."

But the crusaders under the banner of Abolition had tasted too much blood. One of the most malignant and unaccountable assaults against Henry came from right next to him, a chief lieutenant in his own camp: Theodore Tilton's famous "Cleveland letter" ravaged Henry in the pages of Old Bowen's *Independent*. Theodore Tilton, for whom Virtue is all Fire and Combat; his great passion lay in the punishment of transgressors. (And it has always seemed to me, in the light of the unspeakable events that were to follow, that a great significance lies in the fact that the first major quarrel between Henry Ward Beecher and Theodore Tilton concerned Forgiveness.)

They had been more than battle companions, more than friends. At the newspaper's editorial office, while Theodore read proof, Henry would lie down on his chaise, close his eyes, and take one of his famous siestas. Then Theodore would read Henry's articles aloud to him. They were father and son. As Father had asked Henry to be his stenographer in the heresy trial, so Henry asked Theodore to be his stenographer—Henry hired Theodore to come to Plymouth on Sundays, to take down his words from the pulpit and put them into proper form for the press. This practice (like the issue of forgiveness) has long lain in my mind as the index for a problem I was destined to solve, teasing me: what must a "son" begin storing up in his heart, as his pen scratches down endlessly his "father's" words? Is the task itself too over-laden with hidden guilt and awe and unconscious envy—especially if the son sees the task of his life as the articulation of his own words, if he realizes that they must contradict the words he so faithfully records from the leaping tongue of patriarchal flame? Especially so, I presume, in the big-business world of Henry Ward Beecher—he was making twenty thousand dollars a year now in salary, and almost as much from his lectures, articles, and books. The richest preacher in America. The pew rentals at Plymouth were bringing in sixty-five thousand dollars annually—and the collections forty thousand dollars more. How could a young, literary sort of man not be dazzled?—as he sat in the red-and-white majesty of Plymouth, faithfully transcribing the golden tones that melted down into hard cash.

Theodore Tilton is six feet tall, variously called "Apollo" and "Adonis" by his adoring throng. The man wears his blond locks in the leonine style of his mentor; Theodore Tilton, already famous for his rondels, ballads, and triolets (I am frequently pestered by one of his more saccharine successes, the cradle hymn "Baby Bye"). And now that the southern slave class has achieved its freedom, Tilton has thrown himself into the fray for the emancipation of womanhood—he has become an intimate of Mrs.

Stanton, Miss Anthony, and—Isabella Beecher Hooker. There is mischief in it, clear mischief. The papers say that our Theodore has also insinuated his dapper counsel into the very inner circle of advisors who are headlong working to elect Mr. Horace Greeley to the Presidency.

"The Griffin," Eunice, will no longer allow Tilton into her house; she will not set foot in his. I wondered about that, too, wondered what danger she saw, until Henry showed me an epistolary effusion from the young man. Henry said, "Don't you see, Tommy, Eunice is shutting her door on my dearest boy? Look here and tell me why." So I looked at it, and I knew precisely why:

Midnight. Brooklyn,
November 30, 1865

Rev. Henry Ward Beecher,

My Dear Friend, returning home late tonight I cannot go to bed without writing you a letter. Twice I have been forced to appear as your antagonist before the public, the occasions some years apart. After the first I am sure our friendship, instead of being maimed, was strengthened. After this one, if I may guess your heart by knowing mine, I am sure the old love waxes instead of wanes.

Two or three days ago, I know not how impelled, I took out of its hiding-place your sweet and precious letter written to me from England, containing an affectionate message which you wished should live and testify after your death. Tonight I have been thinking that in case I should die first, which is equally probable, I ought to leave in your hand my last will and testament of reciprocated love. My friend, from my boyhood up you have been to me what no other man has been, what no other man can be. While I was a student, the influence of your mind on mine was greater than all books and all teachers. The intimacy with which you honored me for twelve years has been, next to my wife and family, the chief affection of my life. By you I was baptized; by you married; you are my minister, teacher, father, brother, friend, companion. The debt I owe you I can never pay. My religious life, my intellectual development, my open door of opportunity from labor, my public reputation—all these, my dear friend, I owe in so great a degree to your kindness that my gratitude cannot be written in words, but can only be expressed in love.

What hours we have had together! What arm-in-arm wanderings about the streets! What hunts for pictures and books! What mutual revelations and communings! What interminglings of mirth, of tears, of prayers!

The more I look back upon this friendship, the more am I convinced that not your public position, not your fame, not your genius, but just your affection has been the secret of the bond between us. Whether you had been high or low, great or common, I believe that my heart, knowing its mate, would have loved you exactly the same—

Beginning to tremble—"my heart knowing its mate"—Cold Tom was trying to read on, but only wanted to take the letter out of the room, like a dead mouse carried by its tail to the rubbish. I glanced up to see Henry staring, with wet eyes, at an opal.

—Now, therefore, I want to say that if either long ago or lately any word of mine, whether spoken or printed,

*whether public or private, has given you pain, I beg you
to blot it from your memory, and to write your
forgiveness in its place. Moreover, if I should die,
leaving you alive, I ask you to love my children for
their father's sake, who has taught them to reverence
you and to regard you as the man of men.*

*I believe human friendship outlasts human life.
Our friendship is yet of the earth, earthy; but it shall
one day stand uplifted above mortality, safe, without
scar or flaw, without a breath to blot, or a suspicion to
endanger it.*

*And now, good-night; and sweet be your dreams of
your unworthy but eternal friend,*

Theodore Tilton

I gave the billet-doux back to Henry.

He said, "Is it not beautiful?"

I said, "Make sure to keep it."

"Oh," he said, waving his arms, "could I ever
part with it?"

"Just be sure to keep it."

Startled, disappointed, he looked wonderingly
at Cold Tom.

Who thanked the Lord for Eunice.

I thanked Henry, too, for the copy of his newly
published novel. But I let it sit there on a corner of
the desk in my pack-rat office in Elmira, let it sit
there for weeks before I could brave voyage into its
sargasso. *Norwood!* I was unable to fathom, at first,
why my brother should ever fancy that he could—or
should—commit himself to a sentimental romance.
Perhaps he heard a sudden fire-bell in his soul: What
will history think of me when my voice is silent? I
must write. History won't know Henry Ward Bee-

cher through his sermons—those are nothing without my voice and carriage, all personal and present animation—no, I must find characters and action in words to install myself in the heart of posterity. The world-wide success of Hatty's *Uncle Tom* had been a lesson for every Beecher: Harriet was now forever emblazoned in the sky of time. So Henry procured an enormous sum from one Mr. Bonner, a publishing magnate, and then found himself incapable of making good on the deal. Tore up pages as fast as he wrote them. He said to me, "I have dreamed two plots, Tommy, but forgot them as soon as I waked. I began a word-picture of a Jackass this morning and came near writing my own biography."

He had wanted, I believe, to try his chapters out on Theodore Tilton; but the squire was now on a lecture circuit, off in the great West, fully four months of the year. So Henry sweated on alone. I was alarmed enough to raise an eyebrow when he implored, "Give me your best wishes for a good intellectual impregnation, gestation, and delivery" —especially alarmed when I learned that in Theodore's absence, and with Eunice having no time for "novels!" Henry had secured an auditory with Tilton's wife, little Elizabeth Tilton, "Lib," a child-woman, Henry wrote to me, with a bird-like helplessness that made men feel big and strong around her. Cold Tom groaned in Elmira, watching it snow and snow and snow. "I was about in despair," Henry wrote, "and I needed somebody or other that would not be critical, and that would praise it, to give me the courage to go on with it." So, with Theodore gone, Henry took his blotted papers every day to Theodore's wife, to intone his Romance to her.

Snow and snow and yet more snow, the evergreens groaning with their great burdens. Oh, the whole terrible affair began with writing a novel!

I buckled down to *Norwood,* finally, and came to a passage about "a crown of trailing arbutus," which recalled that Henry had found a picture called "The Trailing Arbutus" and took it back to Lib Tilton, and she proudly displayed it on her parlor wall. Isabella had written to me that Susan B. Anthony had been most impressed when Mrs. Tilton showed it off to her. Isabella's letters were thick with sordid detail; she said that Henry had been seen on many occasions with Mrs. T., buying her fancy soaps, perfumes, copies of his sermons, a painting of the Virgin Mary holding the body of Christ (to go with the soap?), several fine mezzotints of Henry himself (to go, I suppose, with the perfume); they raced around in his buggy, for Henry had a team of spanking grays that he adored to send off at a gallop. Belle implored me to go down and "shake some sense into him!" A paragraph in the center page of the *Christian Union* was quite good enough for Belle to cut out and send on—Henry's sermon on The Confession of Adultery:

> With the lurid light of revelation his monstrous wickedness stands disclosed in him—that man ought not to wait so long as the drawing of his breath, if he does the thing that is best he will rise in his place and make confession. Though it be in church, and it break the order and routine of service, he will stand up and say, "Here I am, a sinner, and I confess my sin!" Yes, that is the wise course and you would think so—if it was anybody else but yourself.

The blizzard receded, and I took a breather on my tricycle.

There were passages in *Norwood* where I did hear some old stout bells, passages where I knew Henry was deep in the recollections of his own adolescent conversion:

> I cried out, "My God, why hast thou forsaken me?" What followed I can account for only as a phantasy. Or was it real? Is there still an inspiration? I did not *think*. It was *seeing* rather. The whole Heaven seemed full of ineffable gentleness. I was caught up into it, and felt borne in upon me a sense of God's care for me. For the first time in my life I had a conception of *infinite* love. The psalms rushed before me in which trees, mountains, sun, moon, stars, all nature, were called upon to join in praising God. Before, I had read them as one hears Handel's *Messiah,* in fragments, on a piano. Now it was as I imagine the *Messiah* to have been when thousands of singers and instruments gave it forth in all its grandeur at Westminister Abbey. Everything within me became heroic.

Yes, I said, that's Henry. Not quite a novel, perhaps, but indisputably Henry.

There were passages of a dark and special trouble, a kind of weakening into Gothic sluice. Special anxieties that I could not quite bear to read, for I kept seeing Henry in Lib Tilton's parlor, reading them aloud to her:

> How wondrous are the early days of wedlock, in young and noble souls! How strange are the ways of two pure souls wholly finding each other out; between whom for days and months is going

on that silent and unconscious intersphering of thought, feeling, taste, and will, by which two natures are clasping and twining and growing into each other!

Unconscious intersphering—clasping and twining? Oh, that mine enemy should write a book!, but not my brother, not Henry. "There is a wisdom of feeling as well as of thought"—very well, had I not heard him say much the same to me (and to our own Jamesy, as we sent him to China)? Oh, that's just Henry, always fighting against Father, but now Father would come roaring up out of his grave to smash Henry's pen: In *Norwood* "the intuitions of our sentiments seldom mislead us." And, as if Henry suddenly catches himself in his heresy, he tries to take it back—only to make it worse: "*Moral* sentiments. I warned against passion and sultry ardors." Beware, I thought, beware the man who answers the question that was not asked. And then I was ready to give him up: the hero came to the heroine "as one comes to an altar or a shrine. He left her as one who has seen a vision of angels." And I could see Henry leaving Lib Tilton's house, his papers under his arm, a dazzled smile upon his round, fifty-seven-year-old face.

Henry Ward Beecher was on a little bitty spree—in America, now the land of generals and women. The winter passed reluctantly away, spring flared and settled into summer, and all the while there were rumors, rumors out of Brooklyn—twin sisters from Cranberry Street called upon me in Elmira, their gloves as long as stockings, their eyes darting back and forth, insinuating dainty little questions, dropping innuendos into their tea. They said Mr. Tilton was in Des Moines, and exchanged knowing glances. Then they bundled themselves off to the station in a taxi. In the wash of their hack I pondered, opened *Norwood,* looked for some signs of innocence, and found the sentence, "A hollyhock is a moral and accountable being!" I went out to the side-yard, by the stream, quizzed a hollyhock, and found it—deficient.

As for the liberation of the ladies, Henry had learned a large lesson from Father: if you want to make something new, make it look old. Put a radical idea in conservative dress. Make no innovations; embark on no novel experiments; set up no new standard of morals. Stand on the defensive. Contend for altars and firesides. Rally 'round the standard which our fathers reared: the inheritance which they bequeathed no man shall take from us. True wisdom consists in advocating a course only so far as the community will sustain it.

And so Henry's speeches on Women's Rights take a careful old line: "Surely a woman is better fitted for home who is also fit for something else. No woman is a better guardian and developer of infants for being ignorant. No one is a more tender companion for being weak and helpless." Yes, I thought, the beautiful tactic! Here comes the Fifteenth Amendment, and we'll give our girls the vote for conservative reasons. When women got the ballot they'll be better mothers. Higher purity, higher beauty. Educate them custodians of culture. It's not equal footing—it's taller pedestals!

The feminists must have respectability, and that's why the less progressive, New England Suffragists have gone and picked Henry for their

President—he's a handy affront to Stanton and Anthony and all those radical New Yorkers in the Equal Rights Association. But now the ERA has elected Theodore Tilton their President. So the two outfits are going to work out a compromise; they're convening together, Henry and Tilton both at the chair, and—and little Lib Tilton, Theodore's precious tidbit, as corresponding secretary. Isn't *that* fun? Oh, but truly, none but a sincere, well-meaning man could allow himself to be so used, as Henry is, for no profit to himself—used by such designing females. But that's Henry—all impulse; he's the convolvulus—wants to be running on somebody all the time. When it gets too tiring, he takes refuge in writing a *Life of Christ!*

I studied one of his latest sermons:

"A healthy man in the open air breathes about two thousand cubic feet of air an hour. Our best hospitals make arrangements for about six hundred cubic feet per hour; the schools in the city of Philadelphia—and it is supposed to be a model city—provide for each child one hundred fifty-six cubic feet per hour. In our Brooklyn schools, fifty-nine, forty-five, thirty-nine, and in one disgraceful instance, twenty-four cubic feet are provided for these little wretches that we call our children. If they had been thieves they would have got six hundred in jail. An audience gathered together in ordinary assembly rooms not only have no considerable proportion of that air which they should have—"

Oh well, he must have read it somewhere.

"—ordinarily in about fifteen minutes the fresh air has been all used up once, and will very soon be breathed over twice, three times, four times, five times, and in less than an hour every man, woman, and child in the assembly will have in him something of every other man, woman, and child. It is but very rarely that one sees a person who thinks so well of another that he would like to eat him up. We have a vaporous intimacy with each other's interiors!"

I blinked, startled, and walked around. Vaporous intimacy with each other's interiors?

I had to write him. My scribbled letter asked him if he was straightening his pen for the sex-wars. I dawdled in my irony, and then he wrote right back: "Let Theodore T. and Susan B. go on; only *I* won't quarrel with them, and if you quarrel with me, be prepared to hear me talk to you like a father." Well, there's my irony sent back with a brick. Henry signed his letter, "Truly yours, Tommy, without regard to gender." He added a P.S.—"Don't ask me to be solemn about the woman question. I can't do it." But Hatty was after him, Henry enclosed her letter—

If a woman undertakes to protest she is overwhelmed by a deluge of filth. Thank heaven, Henry, you can speak on this subject with authority. Put Bowen's grief out of your mind. You are, and always have been, blameless, since your youth was as pure as a woman's and the seed of your mother remains in you—

Lord, I thought, Hatty loves to lay it on. But—but—

Q: Bowen? His grief? What's Bowen? The silk merchant, he just owns the *Independent*—he don't control it. Bowen don't care for positions; he cares for profits. Absentee, self-congratulatory benevolence.

And—Q: Why 'blameless'? Why must Hatty—
A: There must be something horribly *behind*.

Then Hatty wrote, "Susan Anthony and those other honest old maids know no more evil than a country minister's horse." Well, that I did like. Hatty's all right. At least she stands with him. But there's Catharine yelling at him from the right—Isabella yelling at him from the left—how can he move, one way or the other, without getting whacked by a sister. I remembered Belle's famous speech when she said that Henry had declared that God was black, Christ was a mulatto, the Devil was white, and that Henry's greatest regret was that he was not born black himself.

And suddenly I was laughing, laughing at Belle, laughing at myself, laughing at Henry, laughing at *Beecher*—there in my little kitchen, laughing my lungs out.

Then the big blast came, as such blasts often do, from Boston. There, at some convention of marginal spiritualist quackery, a visiting New Yorker, Victoria Woodhull, unleashed a thunderbolt that ignited a beacon fire. She shrieked in a hall: "I know of one man, a public teacher of eminence, who lives in concubinage with the wife of another public teacher of almost equal eminence. All three concur in denouncing offenses against morality. 'Hypocrisy is the tribute paid by vice to virtue.'"

And the Beecher Boats were blown to kingdom come.

The Woodhull," As Victoria was so splendidly called, sprang up as the incuba of a treacherous nest of catamounts. Her father, a river-boat gambler, dabbled in counterfeiting; he was a Mediumistic Zealaton, a pettifogger who bartered his little girl away when she was just fourteen to one alcoholic Doctor Woodhull of San Francisco. Vicky and Doc were soon cursed with an idiot boy, and then a girl whom they called Zulu Maud. Victoria made her demure way as an actress in a clairvoyant condition with the "Corsican Brothers." Her sister, Tennie Claflin—or, as she hieroglyphed it, "Tennie C." (though she seemed to me to be in a "border state")—published a rag underwritten by Commodore Vanderbilt, *Claflin's Weekly,* featuring such special numbers as an intriguing "Communist Manifesto" by Mr. Marx and Mr.

Engels. The Woodhull, "considering superior offspring a necessity," commanded her sex to "procreate only with superior men." I don't know if that plank of her platform was loose when she decided to use Theodore Tilton, Boy Romantic, to go after Henry. She said, "The fault with which I charge Henry Ward Beecher is not infidelity to the old ideas, but unfaithfulness to the new."

After her elaborate orations on the Garden of Eden as an allegory of the human body, she went on to describe how she had received the revelation of her true calling: sulking in pantocratic vapors she saw her parlor fill with light and a majestic guardian, clad in a Greek tunic, suddenly appeared unto her, and wrote his name in English letters on the dust of her table: "DEMOSTHENES." I so wished she had dusted. But "Untrammeled Lives!" was her watchword, and when The Good Gray Poet was dismissed from his post in Washington, The Woodhull sprang to Walt's defense; she wore a white tea-rose at her throat, her hair cut brashly short. She and Tennie C. strode from hired hall to hired hall, in their jaunty Alpine hats and mannish jackets; along the furious passage Victoria shed the besotted Dr. Woodhull and "married" one Colonel Blood, a burly veteran of Shiloh (with lead in his leg to prove it), a massive specimen of male aggression, with Dundreary whiskers.

I was filled in on all this by our Belle, who referred to the lady hyena as "My Darling Queen." Isabella proclaimed, "That little woman has bridged with her prostrate body an awful gulf over which womanhood will walk to her freedom." There was apparently a widening schismatic hysteria among the New York ladies. Elizabeth Cady Stanton had to write to Miss Anthony: "Offended Susan: Come right down and pull my ears. I shall not attempt a defense. I have made an awful blunder in not keeping silent on this terrible Beecher-Tilton business. The whole odium of the *scandalum magnatum* has been rolled on our suffrage movement." The battle communiqués magically turned up in the public press.

At which point Sister Catharine interposed her body for The Defense. When I read of it, I felt faint once again from all the bad times and guilty rhythms I had harbored when I played consort on Catharine's western trajectory. But as one sister fell in with the enemy, the "true" sister, dear old Caty, suddenly proved that she had been stoking furnace in our father's fire: Catharine took a ride with Victoria Woodhull in Central Park and concluded, "She is either insane or the helpless victim of malignant spirits." Caty stepped out of the carriage with the words, "Remember, Victoria Woodhull, that I shall strike you dead." And The Woodhull, who keeps getting seized by one of them overwhelming gusts of inspiration, blabbed immediately in her *Weekly,* "I replied to Miss Beecher, 'Strike as much and as hard as you please—only do not do it in the dark so that I cannot know who is my enemy.'"

During those weeks I fairly lived on my tricycle; I pedalled around like a mandarin, chortling in my perspiration, chanting the New Woman's call to arms: "We mean treason! We are plotting revolution!" I thought of installing trailing gunnery on my trike, and offering it to either side as an armored vehicle.

Then, in Manhattan, the pinched and dangerous Mr. Anthony Comstock—what mischief is the right instinct in the wrong head!—worked himself up into a convulsion of civic imbecility and marched upon the dainty charges of the Commodore, catching them in the very act, as it were, with five hundred bound copies of their *Weekly*. Comstock & Co. stuck the ladies with Obscene Matter Through the Mails; the Claflin presses were destroyed, the ladies thrown in Ludlow Street Jail, where bail was set at ten thousand dollars each, sixteen thousand dollars the pair. Mr. William F. Howe, of Howe & Hummel, sprung the ladies—and like rubber they were back in again. In and out of court, in and out of jail—for months. My heart softened along with my brain. Victoria was scheduled to speak at Cooper Institute, though policemen were set in a ring about the place to prevent her; she responded by disguising herself as an Old Quaker Woman, sidling in to see, in a "Friendly" fashion, what the trouble was—then dashed up on stage, dodged behind a pillar, and appeared in full oratorical display with that white tea-rose at her throat. The policemen were too enthralled to do their duty.

The world's over; the principle of reason has departed; we run about the country like the damned, everywhere blundering into the intense inane. The Monstrous is truly funny and profoundly exhausting. This Orgy of Literature—letters, public "cards," categorical statements of denial (stridently affirmed), tricky pamphlets, unbreakable codes, and broken hearts—all delicately fried and served up in butter sauce.

Old Henry Bowen, now the publisher not only of the *Independent* but of the *Christian Union* as well, had an unruly Theodore Tilton on his hands who splashed an editorial in the *Independent* on "Love, Marriage, and Divorce":

Marriage without love is a sin against God—a sin which, like other sins, is to be repented of, ceased, and put away. When love departs, marriage ceases, and divorce begins. This is the essence of Christ's ideas.

Poor Bowen received a storm of letters cancelling subscriptions. Better that, I suppose, than to have the entire citizenry in the courts of connubial malfeasance. So Bowen had no choice; he cashiered Tilton. Henry Ward Beecher counselled the dismissal.

Bowen knew what he was about: he decided to let Tilton and Beecher fight it out. Bowen himself did not much mind who emerged the victor: he could get rid of one or t'other, and possibly both. He even delivered Tilton's letter to Henry (though he later disclaimed knowledge of its contents). A variety of pamphlets and scandal sheets obtained copies of Theodore's epistle, headlining it:

Henry Ward Beecher: I demand that, for reasons which you explicitly understand, you immediately cease from the ministry of Plymouth Church, and that you quit the city of Brooklyn as a residence.

When Henry received the letter, he is supposed to have said, "Why, this man is crazy, this is sheer insanity!" Or he said, according to other pamphlets, "I am in a dream, this is Dante's *Inferno*." Some broadsides had him staggering down a flight of stairs, crying out that he was "on the brink of a moral Niagara—this will kill me!" Knowing my brother as I do, I supposed he could have said any of it, none of it, or all of it. Each exclamation had the

Beecher stamp—which could guarantee authenticity, or could merely indicate that Bowen knew his man. A careful observer, like old Bowen, or an intuitive enthusiast, like young Tilton, merely had to dab his brush in the palette. There are no quiet colors in Henry's rainbow.

A middleman emerged. He was grabbed by this insufferably bookish crowd, and dubbed "Our Mutual Friend." Frank Moulton had been Theodore Tilton's close friend in college, so he was on Tilton's side; but Moulton's wife was one of Henry's devoted female parishioners, who kept pulling her husband over to Henry's side. Caught right in the unblinking eye of the storm, Moulton, a bond tycoon, stepped in to prevent—or to maintain—the whole literary clambake. He called Henry to his home, and got him to dictate a letter:

My dear Moulton: I ask through you Theodore Tilton's forgiveness, and I humble myself before him as I do before my God. He would have been a better man in my circumstances than I have been. I will not plead for myself; I even wish that I were dead. But others must live and suffer. I will die before anyone but myself shall be inculpated.

At the trial it was asked how an innocent man could dictate such words. If Tilton's letter to his "soulmate" had seemed to me like a mouse I would catch by the tail, this was the messy corpse of a woodchuck, and one looks for a shovel. Moulton had called the father and son together, and Henry wailed, "If this goes public I will go out of the world by voyage to some foreign land or by suicide!"

Each week now I would pause to tote the score.

I examined each epistle, each scrap of information, each public horror. I missed Father. I took out the violin and gawked closely at rosewood and gut. I took the fiddle outside and sat with it on my tricycle. "Sheer insanity . . . wild whirl. This will kill me! On the brink of a moral Niagara . . . humble myself before him as I do before my God. . . ." I was inhabiting a brick area on the inner court of a madhouse, and then I had the key to it, the clear and special key for a jammed lock:

Infidelity! It all comes up and breaks down to—to Infidelity. Perhaps only a favorite son of Lyman Beecher could hear the deeper resonances of theological hum in the dainty particulars.

Then the cleansing fire was consumed in the vulgar conflagration: Lib Tilton's diary was published, and she referred to her lost child, her miscarriage, as "a love-babe, it promised." An editor called "love-babe" to the public's attention as "a very curious expression from a woman nearly forty years old and the mother of six children to describe a child begotten in lawful wedlock." Miscarriage or—abortion?—a child bled out of a woman-babe's body—Cold Tom wobbled in converging shadows. I opened *Norwood,* a holy text and Exhibit A:

> No more self-deceiving. No more suffering and misnaming of one's deepest life. No more shame for the heart's best fruit.

Each word a dagger. Misnaming one's deepest life? No more—shame?

In our spiritual ocean Lib Tilton's letters to her husband were caught up in the trawling net: "Oh, my dear husband, may you never need the discipline of being misled by a good woman, as I was by a good man."

Henry is guilty—guilty of such a great deal and such a little thing.

Lib wrote that her "weapons were love, a large untiring generosity, and"— it became a joke in the street, a catchword for sophisticates and a blind slur for playing children—*"nest-hiding!"*

But the "nest" was broke wide open and the eggs were crashing through—which is where Tom Beecher took his stand, watching the eggs fall, amazed at their size and velocity. I had been re-reading Henry's original letter of acceptance to Bowen. Henry wrote that Eunice was "literally giving her very life to aid me and sustain me in my work in the West." In his official announcement to the Indianapolis congregation, he said he had to leave them so as "to save the life and restore the health of my wife."

Domestic devotion—the perfect camouflage for male ambition! I got to go to Brooklyn—my *wife's* life depends on it.

The hypocrite! My heart ganged after The Woodhull. I scoured myself, and recalled how I had cautioned Father to withhold any adverse influence on Henry's prospects. And when I was working myself up into a fury, a sedentary young parishioner of mine, Mr. Loftis, appeared at my rag-tag office downtown, with one of those dreadful pamphlets in his hands. What, Mr. Loftis wondered in his great-coat, was happening to my brother, this man to whom the nation owed the salvation of its soul? I sighed, the sigh of conscious futility; wild horses were bolting, and Thomas Kinnicut Beecher does not mount his tricycle to pursue a runaway team.

Young Loftis, a blighted little tree in his greatcoat, said, "Uncle Alvin told us your father's letter of recommendation was mighty gloomy."

"Yes?"

"Excuse me. I—the committee solicited"—he was like a dunce at the Hartford High School, failing elocution—"the advice of Henry Ward Beecher, the noted Abolitionist—"

Came late, I thought, came very late to the title.

"Uncle Alvin, he sez Mr. Beecher did not respond by mail."

I wasn't quite listening.

"No, everyone was talkin' about your father's letter—it was just gloom all over—and by gum Henry Ward Beecher shows up at the depot."

I still missed it. By gum.

"Uncle Alvin said Mr. Beecher prayed with them, laughed with them, told them the secrets of your life—"

I flared at the upstart Loftis—the secrets of my life—"The secrets of my life?"

"Oh, beggin' pardon, only your grief."

Only my—my grief?—to the elders of Park Church? Livy? Henry told them about Liv—and—

"And now we was all wonderin', since he did such a capital job, he shore convinced us—but these reports are mighty discouragin', to Uncle Alvin, anyway."

Father made me too gloomy—and Henry pulled me out of the slough? And now I should be at my sainted fornicating brother's side?

Young Loftis swayed his grey arm-branches weakly. "This man in the hall out here is hankerin' to get a morsel—"

Man in the hall? Hankerin' for a morsel? I jumped up from my desk to discover a newsbird perched on the bannister, a popinjay of the press, with a match in his mouth and green striped pants.

It is a conspiracy. The Methodist divine who calls "Tom" the rankest of the lot. And then I had two men in my office, two men whose collective ages did not hit fifty, whose eyes ferreted my digs with the cruelty of the eager young.

Henry sent Jamesy to China and Tommy to Elmira—Henry, smiling to an opal—oh, my big brother using Eunice's malarial fevers for his gelid eye on the throne, the slave-selling Pulpit Poppy—no more shame—

What I said then assumed a cold lucidity in type, broadcast throughout a land famished for corroboration of its baser instinct: I said,

> Mrs. Woodhull only carries out Henry's philosophy, against which I recorded my protest twenty years ago.

The confidence men made their grubby exit. I do not remember a pencil and paper, I did not see the words taken down, I have no distinct remembrance of ink on the fiber of wood pulp, no feathered quill flowing on parchment. I took to bed with the ague, and great beakers of beer, finally rising in tumbled furniture to make my helpless course to the post office where among the circulars was a neat note from 124 Columbia Heights, a copy of the words in triple-point type:

> MRS. WOODHULL ONLY CARRIES OUT HENRY'S PHILOSOPHY AGAINST WHICH I RECORDED MY PROTEST TWENTY YEARS AGO.

suitable for framing.

I unfolded it like a map—

1. A copy of the *Gazette,*
2. A note from Henry: *"Et tu, Tomy?"*
3. And a single word from her, a single word from Eunice Bullard Beecher, in her mannish hand: *"Why?"*

Why, indeed, said Tom, pedalling home in—tears, idle tears!

A wife would have shut me up.

Tears are not the overflow of the soul; tears are the oily excess fluid squeezed from a worn-out chamois. On the ferry I stood in the bow and watched a gull swoop like graphite against the westering sun, pure glide and wing-gristle.

A female servant let me in, and I found Henry in his study stretched upon the floor in his shirt sleeves, blue serge trousers, and embroidered slippers.

He turned, saw me, and stumbled up. "Well," he said, "Sir Malapert."

He knew everything—and knew it immediately. I have always and have never been able to understand why people think Henry Ward Beecher is a fool.

His big face was all fatigue. "This scandal is an open pool of corruption. It exhales deadly vapors."

My eyes went down to the Persian carpets glowing there in the firelight.

"Oh, Henry—if—"

"Do you remember, Tommy, at father's heresy trial, the faces of the clergymen?—and so few of them intellectual faces?"

I looked at his.

"The elders were just what forty farmers are supposed to be—except—"

"Except"—I filled in for him—"except stupidity is usually graced with more gravity than good sense."

Henry smiled. As if he were glad to see me. Sir Malapert.

"The Scotch Presbytery." He held up a fat finger. "Q.," he said. "Q: Will the mon tell us in what relation Adam stood to his posterity?"

I waited.

"A?" he said.

"Oh," I said, "Oh—A: In the relation of a federal head."

"Q: What do you mean by a federal head?"

"A: A head with whom God made a covenant for all His posterity."

Henry's sad eyes twinkled. "Maybe a *leetle* too orthodox."

We smiled together.

"MacArthur and"—he snapped his fingers several times, searching—"MacArthur and—"

"Craig?"

"Craig! Yes, Tommy, I've been searching for that name all day. Father Craig was appointed to squeak the questions. The Holy Whine. Some claret? We have no beer."

He lunged around, on those embroidered slippers, to the giant bookcase; he sneaked his big hand back behind some tall volumes. His other hand found glasses and then he poured, stood staring at the claret glasses as if they were color-opiates. The fine color reminded him, as much as it absorbed him, for he turned back to where the bottle came from and handed me a pamphlet, *The Little Red Lounge, or Beecher's Fix.*

Led astray by VENUS' soft delights,
He scarce could rule some idle appetites;
For all we know, since NOAH and the flood,
The best of pastors are but flesh and blood.

I handed it back. "Tilton?"

"Oh, Tommy, no, no—" His hand patted the table.

We sat in silence.

Nobody is with him. I glanced at the dying fire, and the unspoken words were bounding in my head: nobody is *with* him. How can the most popular man in America be alone in his study—the great Temperance man drinking claret, alone?

"So often"—he began, drifted off into silence, and then came back—"so often Theodore would throw himself into some sort of voluminous paper. 'A True Statement.' Bowen and I, we felt the only way to manage Teddy was to let him work off his periodical passion and—and then—"

"And then?"

"Pounce on it and suppress it." Henry's hands became fists, trembling. Then, slowly, they flattened out again.

"I have not understood Bowen."

Henry looked at me sharply, then away. "Oh, he is solemnly brooding over an awful reality." He said the words like a quotation, then said them again, "Not pursuing a phantom, but solemnly brooding over an *awful reality*." Henry's eyes filled—and then he laughed, a great laugh that fairly shook the study.

Then he was almost whispering to himself, "Mrs. Morse wrote to me—Mrs. Morse, Lib's mother, the—the inevitable mother-in-law—she wrote to me—'I don't believe if Theodore's honest debts were paid he would have enough to buy their breakfast; his half-drunken brain is a riot; he is killing her by slow torture; she is in want—actual want.'" Henry fairly declaimed it, in an old woman's voice, then dug back down into a parody of his own: "But I tread the falsehoods into the dirt from which they spring and go on my way rejoicing. The Lord has a pavilion in which He hides me."

I stared at him in the firelight. Henry in firelight.

So Tilton is trying to shield himself and family, but wants justice; Henry is doing the same.

I cannot help my brother except by prayer.

But I protest—I protest against the whole batch and all its belongings. He has said that there is a barbarity of dragging a poor dear child of a woman into a slough. So far as I can see it is he who has dragged the dear child into the slough. And left her there. But I don't believe that, I don't. He is in too much pain.

"Theodore heard I had offered my resignation, and he said, 'Tell Mr. Beecher if he resigns his ministry in this crisis I will shoot him on the street.'"

"And would he?"

Henry smiled.

"Belle wrote to me about Mrs. Stanton and Miss Anthony. It wasn't clear—their quarrel."

"Oh," he fluttered his big hand above the glass, "Suzie B. locked herself in a room with Lib and told Theodore he'd enter over her dead body. And then Susan told Elizabeth Cady Stanton. And then Lib tells Mrs. Morse. That woman, that *woman*—"

"Which? We have them a bit piled up."

"I am at the mercy of the tattle of a crowd of

malicious females. Mrs. Morse—now that's where I was—Mrs. Morse, who writes to me, 'My Dear Son,' and signs herself 'Mother'!—she is animated by violent hatreds, hysterical fits, chronic manias and frenzies—oh, Tommy, she once clutched her husband's throat until he grew black in the face." Henry put his hands around his own large throat, his hands digging at the loose flesh. Then his fingers moved back to brush at the grey strings of his hair. "Theodore said that when she departed the house she thrust her parasol like a rapier in his breast, breaking off the handle." Henry was up now, up from his chair, the sublime mimic, doing the crazy lady: "She came at him with a carving knife and threatened to cut his heart out. 'You infernal villain—this night you should be in jail, your slimy, polluted, brawny hand curses everything you touch. I shall publish you from Dan to Beersheba'!"

He never can survive this. It is not Niagara. It is the desert.

Eunice Bullard Beecher stepped quietly into the room and said to Thomas Kinnicut Beecher, "I have had a bed prepared."

I rose. Eunice, her hair absolutely white, a braid of perfect ivory, came and looked at me and kissed me. We regarded each other for a moment, she touched Henry's shoulder, and went away.

"She will not allow Mr. Tilton in the house?"

"In the house?" Henry said. "She has not spoken to Theodore in eleven years. He says, 'I have never had so relentless an enemy.'"

"Good."

"Good?" He looked at me.

I looked back. "You know nothing on earth."

He smiled. "It's the password to Heaven." He rolled it to me like a marble.

"Well . . ."

"They tried to warn me. Bob Bonner of the *Ledger*—"

"Where *Norwood* appeared," I said, and could not resist adding, "along with Fanny Fern's raptures."

"With Edward Everett, too. It's just a story paper, Tom."

"But you don't much like being coupled with Fanny Fern."

"Coupled with—"

"Please excuse me. You were trying to tell me something."

"Oh yes," he said, re-animated, "Robert Bonner wrote to me, here, Tommy, I have the letter"—he went to his desk again, and found it, and handed it over:

The Rev. Henry Ward Beecher:

Some of your so-called friends (I allude particularly to Tilton) have in a Pecksniffian way been regretting that you are on the decline. Tilton has said to me that you reached the culminating point in your career when you were in England. I can only say (and I will stake my life on it) that Tilton is not a real friend of you or yours. If he is, he has a queer way of showing it. I would not mention a personal thing like this, did I not consider it my duty as your friend to do so.

I read it slowly, and handed it back. "He is your friend."

"Oh, Theodore has—"

"No, Henry, *Bonner.*"

"Oh, yes—oh, yes."

"Henry, how can you misjudge or—or not notice—do you not know who is close to you?"

"They *all* are!"

"But Henry—"

"That was the idea! When I designed the church. It was a radically new design—the appearance of a closeness."

"The appearance?"

But he was off again: "Dr. Storrs called a council. Do you remember, Tommy?—Father's trial—he said, 'We can whisk this Council down the wind! We can set them all agog!'"

I nodded.

"So with me. So with me. The pew sales— 'Beecher's Auction,' they call it—$59,430! What do you think of that for panic prices?"

"I think I am at a horse sale."

His arm swooped out as if to deliver a blow, then he slapped my face with a pat-pat.

"At the Council, men with pistols, men with pistols were after Moulton. 'You are a liar, sir.' Three thousand voices shout 'Aye' and Moulton shouts 'Nay.' And we were lifted up, 'Praise God from whom all blessings flow'—with cries of 'Iago!' punctuating the—the—did you say 'horse sale'?"

We are not talking to each other. We are being Beecher.

Silence again. Then: "I have letters—letters from presidents of Colleges and Universities, from Bishops, from Senators—they all implore me, 'Stop doing twice as much as any mortal should attempt.'"

"Yes."

"But the others—the others—they call upon me to commit suicide. A horrible deluge in the public prints, on the platforms, in the cars. Lampoons, booklets, skits, mountains of abuse, and scorn, and ridicule, and rage! Look, Tommy—look—" Henry stomped to the other end of the bookcase, bent down to a pile of newspapers and pamphlets and magazines on the Persian carpet. He picked up one of the tabloids and read, "'Mr. Beecher is at most the friendly duck that incubates the egg of destiny; he is not for a moment to be mistaken for the royal bird that lays it.'" Henry nodded at me, slyly. "Well, I rather like that one. Yes, I like it."

The duck in the nest—nest-hiding. I almost uttered it.

"But Tommy, when three thousand people say you are innocent, you *are*. That's my emancipation. The abolition of my slavery to this vicious system. It can be, it can be my freedom from bondage."

How can one feel anything but—scorn? How dare he? My blood resented it.

Your family is no help. Family is who you are.

Silence. Claret. Silence. Henry's desperate voice, in control; his voice like a carefully navigated tunnel: "The people watch me—narrowly—as a mouse is watched by a cat."

And I saw him suddenly, my big brother at twenty, lounging around a porch until a schoolmate said, "You *magnetized*?" Henry said to the vigilant, "I just love to hear your mother talk."

"And Belle—our Isabella—she is threatening to invade my pulpit, to read to the congregation some trumped-up 'confession'"—Henry pronounced the word like an obscenity—"a *confession* of my intimacy with Lib."

"Invade your pulpit?"

"Hatty, faithful Hatty, attends service front and

center, stationed there to grab Isabella, to throw her out—Hatty who can barely move herself. What shall I do, Tommy? Is there no end of trouble and complication? What is the condition of a man who gets such communiqués from a member of his own family—?"

And then we were both frozen with it, a terrible flaming blunder, Tom's pronouncement to the press—

Henry said it: "Against which you registered your protest twenty years ago."

I stood there.

He started toward me, and I turned away.

"Tommy, it will all be better by and by."

Oh, how I hate the world. And hated it that night when Henry invited me along to Prayer Meeting at Plymouth. On my way in I was handed a pamphlet by a Mrs. Augusta Moore, her privately printed word-chromo of Plymouth proceedings; she said that if we casually think Henry Ward Beecher is a ploughboy, or a butcher in minister's clothes, we know not his torpedo-like heart, his face like the angels' faces we have seen in dreams. In his flurry he stands forth as Boanerges, a mountain in a winter storm. Mingling in his tones, Mrs. Moore hears "reminders of Niagara, and of the crash of thunder; while his flashing eyes and changing features have the effect of lightning, and his gestures represent the rushing wind." I sat in the crowded, candle-lit darkness of Plymouth, and I couldn't help thinking what *Mr.* Moore thought. "Then, while you are yet thrilling to the sweep of the storm, you are melted to tears by sorrow, or some longing of magic tenderness of a mother's cradle hymn." *Mr.* Moore, let me ask you again, in all seriousness, should Henry affect your good wife so? "But his imagination is so rich and strong, his flow of language so great, and his heart beating like a great hammer in his breast, that volcanic heart, he is occasionally like a man who has struck his foot so hard against a stone, that, to save himself from falling on his face, he needs must run awhile, though every step be upon vipers." (I especially liked that one, Henry hotfooting it through sarpents.) "One is inclined to smile at the wag of his head when he is about to clinch an argument; the shake of his elbows and his knees, when he knows that he has you penned; the eagerness with which he seizes upon that devoted handkerchief when he is about to 'charge'; the strength with which as he commences his tilt, he turns his hand-palm towards his chair and back towards the desk, leaning on knuckles and thumb, one foot crossed over the other, and supported upon its toe."

Mr. Moore, I implore you: Rescue your Augusta from this spiritual poltroon.

Then Henry was up there, sprawled on his throne, waiting for some inspiration from the faithful. A hush was upon us, and he gradually moved himself to a hypo of reassurance:

"LEARNED PREACHING HAS BECOME TOO DAINTY to walk among facts; it chooses to fly among principles. Such a preacher would work up the Gospel like a man who would tie ribbons on an oak to make it pretty—or suggest amendments to Niagara Falls. That preacher's God is in a temple—mine everywhere. He worships an abstract thought, an idea, not a Living Being. My God lived in Palestine—but he lives now in every meadow. The Bible is to religion what botany is to gardens. God does not live in a book. I am not ashamed to admit that I feel a positive relationship with every living being. Discourses on doctrine—giving stone to those who want bread. Oh, it was a poor exchange that the Puritan made when he bargained off imagination for logic, emotion for metaphysics!"

I thought to myself, the man is skipping rocks on a lake; children hand the flat stones to him, and he lets fly:

"I FEEL when the Calvinist talks about religion as I should feel if my mother were dead and I saw a surgeon using her body for anatomical demonstrations. And no man ever forgets his mother, though her breast was granite, and her kiss frost."

I winced.

But now Henry was off and running in the candlelight: "JUST YESTERDAY I met an old man, a tar, in the street; his features seemed less like a family of relations and more like chance travellers at an inn, put up together for the night." Henry rises, goes into a trance, and comes up the tar: " 'Skates broke, eh?—No?—Gun out of order? Traps gone?' " Henry has magically acquired, in this harlequinade, a wooden leg, and of course we are transfixed, witnesses to the divine energy in the idiom of human personality: " 'Well, what is it, your reference?' " Reverence/Reference—Henry has heard his joke before, but now we hear it as the cry of a delighted child. " 'No, haven't been to prayer meetin', had my dose last week. Have to keep tryin' the pumps. Come, what is it? Don't keep an old fellow with his anchor neither up nor down. But boys will be boys. The only jolly folks in this world are young folks that ain't good for nothin' yet, and old folks that's past doin' much. All the rest of the world is livin' in a pucker and a fume!' "

This world—sighs.

Henry's a drunkard, a wood-cutter, a black-smith, and there was a silly instant there when he was letting go of the old sailor—was I the only one to see it?—a truly fine touch, almost unknown to Henry himself: getting rid of the quid, he wiped his fingers on the back of his coat before he offered the good right hand of fellowship—wiped his fingers on the back of his coat.

Q: Such levity in the house of God?
A: God made man to laugh. Laughter has more power to send Evil into annihilation than twenty years of grim and solemn argument.

"AS A CHILD I wanted to be a Christian. I went about longing for God as a lamb bleating longs for its mother's udder. Billy, my favorite playmate, died. At intervals for days and weeks I cried and prayed for Billy. There was scarcely a retired place in the garden, in the woodhouse, in the carriage house or in the barn that was not a scene of my crying and praying. But what did the school tell me to spell my grief?" And suddenly Henry is his teacher, he is that school-marm staring through her spectacles: " 'Now Henry, "a" is the indefinite article, you see, and must be used only with a singular noun. You can say *a man*, but you can't say *a men*, can you?' " Now Henry is himself as a little boy: " 'Yes, I can say *amen* too. Father says it always at the end of his prayers.' "

The man seated behind me enjoys that. So do all those around me. People are so ready to be happy. Especially in clumps.

" 'Now come, Henry, don't be joking. Decline *he*. Nominative, *he,* possessive, *his,* objective, *him*.

You see, *his* is possessive. You can say "his book" but you can't say *him book.*'" And Henry Ward Beecher is himself a wonderingly shrewd child: " 'Yes, I do say *hymnbook* too.'"

That man behind me chuckles again. Prayer meeting? Sideshow! Oh, damn! And Henry—the man charged with improper and criminal behavior, debauchery and sexual commerce—he has got himself in that schoolroom now, and he wants to sit a spell. He's the haughty mistress who turns to composition. " 'O Billy, write about something that you know about, write about your father's farm.' And so, being goaded to his task, William writes: 'A cow is a useful animal. A cow has four legs and two horns. A cow gives good milk. I love good milk. William Bradshaw.' Ah, but the mistress looks over his shoulder, and says, 'Pooh! Your father will think *you* are a cow. Here, give me that composition, I'll fix it.' And she does: 'When the sun casts off the dusky garments of the night, and appearing o'er the orient hills, sips the dewdrops pendant from every leaf, the milkmaid goes afield chanting her matin song. . . .'"

People are smiling, as if to a whimsical piece on the clarionet. The mountebank, the Sexual Fraud, the Free Lover is in Nature now, opposing *belles lettres* and remembering a day in Indiana when "A heavy rain and flash-flood turned a ravine behind my house into a torrent. I sallied forth to rescue a dog stranded—that large but young dog had walked along, hoping to cross dry-footed, till he came to an abrupt termination, and his courage failing him, he had crouched down and lay trembling and whining on a rapidly shrinking island, afraid to go back or to venture into the water. I fastened together two tubs, made me some oars, and then poled my raft-tubs up to the rescue; and, getting alongside, tried to coax him to come aboard, but his courage was all gone. He looked up wistfully, but stirred not. 'Well, you coward, you shall come aboard!' said I, and seizing him by the skin of the neck, I hauled him onto the raft, which instantly began to sink. It was buoyant enough for a man, but not for a man and a lubberly dog. As the stupid thing would not stir, I had to. There is no end of things gone by; they rise at every point; and one walks encompassed with memories which accompany him through the living streets like invisible spirits. In any event, the tub was upset, and I spent the rest of the morning lazying around drifting in the hot sun."

I joined in with the crowd, smiling at the spectacle of Henry Ward Beecher floating all morning in the hot sun, having failed to save a cowardly dog.

But "Water" encompasses "Fish," so Henry had to catch one; he strode away from his great chair and did a little mime: he baited his hook, cast his line, moved downstream, cast again, then felt a strike!, began to play the plucky trout, moved down the bank, thought he felt the line go slack, then maneuvered more carefully, began to pull, pull—and a man about a dozen pews down from me suddenly shouted, "By God, I think he's got him!"

A wave of delighted laughter rolled around the crowd and up to rest on Henry's face glowing in the candlelight. Then there was a pause, so that Henry could acknowledge with a custom inspector's frown the face of the man who had said "By God" in God's House, and we hushed, and he smiled, and we felt good again.

Oh, damn the world. It lost a great comedian

when Henry Ward Beecher saw the light and heard the call. Joyfully he debases the Christian pulpit. Plymouth is "Beecher's Theatre"—and Henry has said: "If you would pervert the taste—go to the Theatre. If you would imbibe false views—go to the Theatre. If you would be infected with each particular vice in the catalogue of Depravity—go to the Theatre." Well, here we are. And the cowardly dog and the game trout have swung him to Recreation.

"BE A HARP IN AIR—let all things reach forth to touch your strings for joy. Today has been a goblet day. The rose is a floral nightingale; dandelions are golden kisses."

He went on that way, went on and on, giving the people what they wanted. When it was over, a deadly maudlin vapor sat around me and unravelled like gauze. Going out, I at last came to the place in the receiving line where I had to shake my brother's hand—he was standing there the focus and apogee of Glory. What he said to me made me angry, embarrassed, and ashamed—but, at the same time, I thought of what I had said in the newspaper, that terrible proclamation, and I thought, no, I fear Henry Ward Beecher is not Charade, not when he locked eyes with me, broke away from a brace of old sisters, grabbed me in a bear hug, and his voice pealed out a multitude of sins, a bank of greenbacks, a celestial meadow—

"Glorious God, it's my long-lost brother Tommy!"

Then he introduced me to a textile king, whose windows were not agates; no, that man's windows, his eyes, glowed behind shutters, his groping little wife a mauve distraction.

I walked back to the house alone. For some reason I thought of a time long ago, in Hartford, when I tormented a child; I told her the story of Solomon holding up the baby and asking that it be cut in half—and I asked a little girl with a broken tooth, "What if the real mother had said, 'Go ahead, cut it in half'?" The girl's face clouded; she chewed her lip and looked away from me as if I were a criminal. Which I was. We all know the "true" mother is the *good* mother. Virtue is Blood. We may grow up to disbelieve it; but ask a child, ask five children, ask a hundred children, ask Irish children—there is not a child on this earth—the story itself is the answer, the very telling of it, not what you see every day. Time stops. Hear that?—'tis the soul attentive. You believe what you *listen to*.

Upon his return from the church office next morning, Henry sat fidgeting, fidgeting. He said he wanted to walk. So we did, in a great park, the two of us. Along an ice gate of barren sycamores, shuffling on crusty ground, Henry grumbled, "My life's work—to end abruptly and in disaster. My fellow worker dispossessed of his eminent place and influence. I had counselled it."

Henry is feeling sorry for a man who is suing him for one hundred thousand dollars—the man who is charging him with the criminal debauchery of his wife! Henry is feeling sorry for that man.

If it is not macabre, it is surely a miracle.

My flesh was crawling in the winter air.

Henry stationed himself on ice. He ran his fingers through his grey limp hair—a most mangy adulterer—and he spoke, he spoke there in the

January Gethsemane: "To say that I have a church on my hands is simple enough, Tommy—but to have hundreds of men and women pressing me, each one with keen suspicion, or anxiety, or zeal—to see tendencies which, if not stopped, would break out into ruin"—Henry was preaching, preaching to an empty house—"to stop them without seeming to do it—to prevent anyone questioning me—to meet and allay prejudices against Theodore, which had their beginning years before this—to keep serene as if I were not alarmed or disturbed—to pass sleepless nights, and yet come up fresh and full for Sunday"— his heart came pouring out, pouring out—"all this may be talked of, but the real thing cannot be understood from the outside. Not its wearing and grinding on the nervous system. If my destruction would place Theodore all right, I'd be willing to step down and out. No one can offer more than that. That I do offer."

"No. No, do not offer it."

He scanned the great bone branches of the sycamores. "I do not think anything would be gained by it. I should be destroyed, but he would not be saved."

"Exactly. So—you see your way clear."

He turned slightly away. "Eunice and the children would have their future clouded. In one point of view I could desire the sacrifice on my part. Nothing—nothing, Tommy—could possibly be so bad as the horror of the great darkness in which I now spend so much of my time. Life would be—oh, well, pleasant—if I could see re-built that which is shattered. But to live in anxiety, remorse, fear, despair—and yet to put on all the appearance of serenity and happiness—it cannot, it cannot be endured much longer—"

I wiped my runny nose, trembled till I ached. I was not listening any more. I had heard too much. Far across the ground a man was sporting with a large dog. A scene, a pencil sketch.

Grief—it steals up like a thief, stays like a guest, and with most modest objections always seems to show up for supper.

"I do love your cap, Tommy—I would ask you for it, were I not to lose it on you."

We made snowballs and threw them at sycamores, like lonely boys afraid to go home. I cannot slow the drums of blood; they beat, beat smartly in frigid air. We are monsters of cunning and ignorance. In bed, a woman chuckles, chuckles in the swarm of her arms, her hair like jonquils, the convulsive reaching of her belly—oh Lord deliver—

Henry whispered close to me, as we stood in the empty wind-whip of snow, "When I first arrived in Brooklyn the *Police Gazette* was hounding John Newland Maffitt, the great evangelist, hounding him—on the charge of seducing a parishioner. The step-daughter, I think, of a Judge in Brooklyn Court. "And Maffitt's heart—Tommy, his heart burst during the scandal—literally burst. A physician testified at the autopsy."

Take my cap, brother. Take my cap.

Henry Ward Beecher, standing on the ice: "I said to myself, Never to me. Never to me."

We made a turn at a frozen little waterfall and headed back. He muttered, "Clearly, the *Gazette* was purveying salacious material. Just to sell papers. And pretending all the while to be crusading against wickedness."

The rooftops of Brooklyn! Whenever I'm with Henry I feel like a character in a play.

"All my past record will be wiped out—not the

slave auction, not Manchester, not Lincoln—just—
Lib." He stopped me, put his hand on my shoulder,
and scraping with his right foot, he asked, "Tommy,
what can I do?"

Your face is—fat. Finally it is fat.

"The slightest indication of weakness," he said,
"is a confession on my part."

I put my hand up on his. "Say it again, do say it
once again."

"But—what did I say?"

I smiled.

"Tommy, what did I say?"

"Q: What should I do?"

Henry caught it then, caught it in the rigid wind.
"A.—A: The slightest indication—of weakness—is a
confession on my part."

"Done."

He turned. "Angry voices come to me as rude
winter winds roaring through barren trees. The
winds will die. The trees will live." He stood there,
sighed, and said, "Tommy, I must be alone for a
minute or two." He walked slowly away from me,
walked across the ice and snow, walked up to stand
atop a little hill.

And I said to myself, mocking Scripture: Look
at this sorrow that has come upon Christian people.
Behold! The great wolf has been in the fold for years,
robed in sheep's clothing and stealing the greatest
virtue of life from the most tender lambs. Oh,
Beecher! How could you thus conduct yourself?

But looking at him on that little hill I suddenly
saw him as a boy, I beheld Henry the boy, standing
atop a haystack, Henry wearing those blue goggles
that he found somewhere, Henry the boy mounting
his airy perch and beginning his sermon to school-

mates and neighbor-children, he used to articulate words, simply a jargon of word-sounds; with rising and falling inflections he was Father. The rotund phrasing, the sudden descent into solemnity, the sweeping paternal gesture, the upbrushing of the hair—Henry had Father, had him completely—and ended up tumbling down the haystack. Blue goggles, topaz, turquoise—the boy destined to lead the perishing millions of America:

Octamagolee, gazalee gazump, de yump da ray yahoo!
Ink-ta-mink, de rump, de ray yahoo. Jewsy woosey, bibble bible bobble marsh narden, straiden marsh narden, genelums and lewdlies, there rose we go!

Henry the boy on the haystack—and now Henry standing desolate on the snowy hill. At last he turned and walked back. He had seen me watching him, and looked straight at me. He said softly, "Tommy, you have the kindest *eyes*."

THIS TRIAL IS MORE FAR-REACHING in its consequences than any case ever tried in this country. Its effect will be felt in every home in America, nay, in all Christendom. The consequences will reach to the very foundations of society."

That's what the prosecuting attorney claimed.

"WHEN HENRY WARD BEECHER said, 'This will kill me, this will kill me!' he uttered no denial. He was not responding to a charge of 'improper advances.' For Henry Ward Beecher to be innocent you have got to blot out the English language. 'I humble myself before you as I do before my God'—those are the words of a man who knows he is guilty. 'He would have been a better man in my circumstances than I have been'—those are the words of a guilty man. 'Her forgiveness I have'—if he were not guilty, he would not need forgiveness. You cannot forgive a crime that was not committed. When, in 1863, Mr. Beecher faced the mobs of Liverpool and Manchester, his praises rang throughout this broad land for his bravery, his fearlessness, and his courage—bold as a lion—but when he returns to Brooklyn, where he is all powerful, he is a coward. It is the cowardice of conscious guilt. The bravery he manifested in England was the bravery of truth—conscious truth! What is it that now makes him a coward? Conscious guilt! A million false accusations could not frighten that man. But one Tilton, with the truth, and he is a coward. When conscious of his innocence, he knows no fear and can face any danger, but now he says, 'Do with me what you choose, sacrifice me, anything—I deserve it, I *deserve* it!' "

So said Theodore Tilton's counsel, General Roger A. Pryor, who had served in the Confederate Army and had since become one of the leading machine politicians in New York. Henry's battery of attorneys was led by William M. Evarts, the defender of the Savannah pirates, the same Evarts who had faithfully counselled President Johnson through the agonizing ordeal of impending impeachment. He is compared frequently to Henry Clay. Indeed, the arrangements in Brooklyn Civic Court gave off an odor of old political quarrels and new patronage deals. Those eager spectators who were turned away from the courtroom filled the local saloons. Through the court windows I could see them bustling along the icy streets and into the bars. The audience was full of congressmen, ambassadors, social lions, and a mighty phalanx of Plymouth supporters, all scrambling for seats. The *Tribune* alone sent ten reporters to cover the trial. Opera glasses were hawked by vendors, the spriest of which tribe was an old gentleman who capered along the aisles with massive trays of ham sandwiches and mince pies. The Beecherites had sent abundant floral tributes to turn the hall of justice into a veranda: violets vied with lilies—in profusion; the chaste camelia was everywhere in contrast with the petals of the "red, red rose." I sat a few rows behind Henry, Eunice, and two of their sons; Edward was somewhere; Hatty stationed herself in the front. When Henry was charged with "criminal relations," I morbidly inspected the family.

Mr. Evarts, all in brown tweed, spent a day and a half on his praises of Henry, then turned to the accuser: "It becomes now my unpleasant duty to invite you, ladies and gentlemen, to consider for a moment who and what is Theodore Tilton. The plaintiff in this case presents the most impressive instance that has ever come within my observation of the remorseless power and the destructive effect of a single absorbing master passion. An all-dominating selfish egotism is the basis of his character. Beginning life as a reporter, he was brought into contact with great orators and public men, and he early resolved to devote himself to a public career. The art of appearing well and sounding well was the art he sought—a dangerous pursuit for one already strongly predisposed by constitutional vanity to consider life a drama and himself its hero. And so Theodore Tilton fell in with gay, fascinating people, who considered themselves free from the conventional restraints of society, and little by little he slid into their ways of thinking. His unbalanced vanity was not proof against the wine of dangerous theories when presented by the hand of the flatterer. With Theodore Tilton, to calculate the depths of an abyss is to plunge headlong into it."

Mr. Evarts was a kind of austere music, a man at the meridian of his life—what would someday become gloom, I decided, was now the glow of burnished amber.

"Tilton denounced the marriage relation as a remnant of effete civilization. His remedy for the evils of marriage was easy divorce, leaving parties as free to dissolve the relation as they were to enter into it. He denies that he is a free lover, but Victoria Woodhull, the apostle of Free Love, asks for no greater social freedom than this. And when opposition sprang up about him, at last Theodore Tilton was forced to realize that his world was crumbling beneath his feet, and Theodore Tilton—fell—fell from an eminence seldom attained by men of his age—fell to the very bottom. And he beheld afar off the man who had been his early friend and patron, but whom he had long regarded as his rival, standing firm and erect, his influence widening and deepening, and his hold on public favor becoming more and more permanent and secure. A man fed by inordinate vanity can never awake to a sane, reasonable estimate of himself. Failure and disappointment never lead such a man to self-examination, but excite in him only bitterness, rage, and malice. With him it is never his own folly and importance that have impeded his advance, but some malevolent power has interfered. In the blindness of his rage, Theodore Tilton persuaded himself that the sole cause of his overthrow was *Beecher!* The one man who had prevented him from reaching the topmost summit of fame was *Beecher!* So one resource was left to him. If he had not the power to rebuild, he still had the power to destroy. If he could not be famous, he could be infamous, and he preferred infamy to oblivion. Mr. Beecher long had been his friend and the intimate friend of his wife. That friendship he could pervert; he could make himself the author and the central figure of the most famous scandal of modern times. But no mere words can do justice to this man; none but an artist could make a portrait of the man as he is, could bring out his real character before mankind; and, ladies and gentlemen, that portrait has been painted, and by one of the greatest artists the world has ever known. If any of you ever visit the beautiful city of Milan, you will find that, next to its magnificent cathedral on which thousands of saints and angels stand carved in heavenly white, in the attitude of silent prayer, the pride and glory of that city is in the humble refectory of an ancient monastery, upon the wall of which, four hundred years ago, the illustrious Leonardo da Vinci painted his inspired picture of the 'Last Supper'—a picture, the colors of which are too rapidly fading, but the fame of which will never die. And, ladies and gentlemen, in the most striking portrait of that group of disciples, you will recognize the startling likeness between the sharp and angular face, the cold and remorseless eyes of Judas Iscariot and the same features in his legitimate successor— there, on that consecrated wall, the portrait of Theodore Tilton has stood, waiting, waiting for his birth four hundred years—"

The courtroom was rocked with such applause and shouting that Judge Neilson banged his gavel, banged it repeatedly, crying, "Mr. Evarts, please stop—please stop, Mr. Evarts."

I looked at Theodore Tilton, who was making notes. He looked to me more like a Sphynx than Judas. A Sphynx in an olive coat, white pants and white vest. Some rows away sat Mrs. Tilton, heavily veiled.

"The incontinence of clergymen! It is such a common charge—a charge, whether there is guilt or not, is almost sufficient to blast the usefulness of any minister, however respected, however beloved. Mr. Beecher is hardly the first. The enemies of St. Athanasius, St. Francis de Sales, Fenelon, Archbishop of Cambray, Judicious Hooker (who remained 'dumb as the dead,' though innocent as a babe, for six years of bitter anguish). John Wesley suffered such a charge to pass without any public reply for twenty years, and was driven out of Georgia. But what is the use of an honorable life if it is no barrier to false accusation? Indeed, heroism counts *against* this man—as Mr. Pryor has already pleaded. But look to Plymouth Church, where Mr. Beecher has been known for a quarter of a century; look to Plymouth, standing solid!"

Applause, solid.

Judge Neilson let it play.

On it went, through the barren weeks of January. I would fly to the station on Friday nights, make it to Elmira for the meetings of my Park Church committees, preach the Sabbath service, and then board the cars to return to Brooklyn. My congregation saw no delinquency in my procedure; indeed, it was quite the reverse—"Go to your brother in his time of need," they said, "*we* can manage here, *you* be with your brother."

And since Henry and Eunice were clearly intent

on making a display of family solidarity, I kept coming, joining in the Beecher parade every morning from Columbia Street to the courthouse.

Frank Moulton proved a resolute and imperturbable witness—he had amassed all the crucial documents in the case, the endless apocrypha. As I watched the cool customer on the stand I kept asking myself, "Why—why had Henry so trusted him?" Moulton, the man who was saying, "Mr. Beecher is not a safe man to dwell in a Christian community"; Moulton, the red-haired and red-moustachioed man who was saying that when Henry cried out, "I shall die of it," that he, Moulton, felt that "it shows only a selfish faith in God to go whining into Heaven." Frank Moulton said that his wife, Emma, implored him: "Frank, do not state the facts. Let Mr. Beecher do it. Give the old man another chance."

I looked at Henry; he was waving a rose under his nose.

"Mr. Beecher asked me," Moulton said calmly—as if giving a verdict on a novel brand of champagne—" 'What can I do?' And I replied, 'I don't know. I am not a Christian, I am a heathen, but I will try to show you how well a heathen may serve you.' "

Well, now the heathen was serving him, all right; under reminder of oath he said that Henry had prayed to God to help him stop his sexual relations with Lib Tilton.

Mr. Evarts: "Did he say 'sexual'?"
A: "Yes."
Q: "He used that term?"
A: "I have heard him use a worse term."

"But," Mr. Evarts turned away from the witness to face the courtroom, "in the presence of three men Mr. Tilton said he charged Beecher with improper advances. Would he have dared to turn suddenly about and charge adultery? What we have is plain as day. Henry Ward Beecher humbly asked Mr. Tilton permission to go and see Mrs. Tilton at the conclusion of the accusation. Mr. Tilton said he had a written confession from his wife—but Mr. Beecher has never seen it—we have never seen it—the world has never seen it. We have only the retraction. Henry Ward Beecher went from his interview at Moulton's house to the sick wife of Theodore Tilton, and he there confronted her with the accusations that he had received from her husband. She wrote—and we do have this letter, ladies and gentlemen—" Mr. Evarts held it up to read to the transfixed courtroom:

December 30, 1870

Wearied by importunity and weakened by sickness, I gave a letter inculpating my friend Henry Ward Beecher, under assurances that it would remove all difficulties between me and my husband. That letter I now revoke. I was persuaded to it—almost forced—when I was in a weakened state of mind. I regret it, and recall all its statements.

(Signed) E. R. Tilton

I desire to say, explicitly, Mr. Beecher has never offered any improper solicitations, but has always treated me in a manner becoming a Christian and a gentleman.

(Signed) Elizabeth R. Tilton

Here Mr. Evarts paused, and put down the letter, carefully, upon the defense counsel table. "Ladies and gentlemen, that letter of retraction furnishes conclusive evidence of the nature of the charge. You see that she does not retract a charge of adultery. There is no allusion at all to the offense of adultery. It is a retraction of improper solicitations. Do you believe, ladies and gentlemen, that Henry Ward Beecher would have been satisfied with a retraction of anything less broad than the charge? If you're charged with adultery you don't go down to a sick woman and ask to be released from a rumor of improper advances. You know it don't make sense."

And they knew, the dignitaries and social climbers and potentates. They knew they were at a *matinee*. The morning *Herald* could "recall no one event since the murder of Lincoln that has so moved the people. Through all the offices of City Hall and County Court, in the shops, in the saloons, in the parlors and kitchens, one hears nothing but Beecher and Tilton, Tilton and Beecher, the livelong day and far into the night."

A little less than participant, a little more than spectator, Thomas Kinnicut Beecher performed a sort of auxiliary role—sometimes running ahead of the wagon, to clear the road, sometimes straggling along in the rear collecting whatever had been accidentally cast overboard and needed to be reclaimed. Along with Edward and Hatty I spent my evenings at Henry's house, talking with the stream of innumerable callers who took it upon themselves to offer help and condolence. One night towards the end of February I found myself with an ancient graduate of Yale, a skinny gentleman with thick

eyeglasses who seemed immensely pleased that I
had studied with Taylor—and who wanted to offer
Henry (for the moment stuck with an alderman and a
grocer) assistance in this pesky matter of nest-
hiding. Now stationed as a Federal Judge in the
Northwest, he had prepared a document which he
proceeded to put into my hands:

> Whatever nest-hiding is, two years ago I led a
> party of friends out to Yellowstone Park, and
> one morning they took a shot at an eagle in a
> cottonwood. That evening, returning to the
> cottonwood, we found mother eagle dead in the
> nest, her eaglets still alive, protected beneath
> her. She had taken her death-wounds in silence,
> and covered her young to the last. That was
> nest-hiding, and that was what Mrs. Tilton tried
> to do, using love, forgiveness and secrecy con-
> cerning the wounds which were daily inflicted
> upon her.

When I had finished this urgent bulletin from the
great outdoors, I looked up to see the old man
regarding me with an anxious, hopeful look somewhere back there behind his spectacles, behind his
eyes; I thanked him on behalf of the family, and said
that I knew Henry would be pleased.

Which he was. Though he did not have time to
see all those who hung about the house; "I haven't
been down to the shore to look at the waves," he
said, "but I've heard 'em roar." The *Times* had
posted a reporter each evening on the street, for it
had been rumored that the Beecher household was
being frequented by a "mystery lady." Which was
true enough, given Catharine.

After the rest of them had retired upstairs, I would sit by Henry's study window, as I sit by my own study window in Elmira, to watch the night and the snow. I fish behind the books for the claret and sprawl in the moonlight, in a mellow mood—lost in the immense spectacle of what was passing over us like a madman's reverie. I would dream a little, and see them all—Theodore, little Lib, Henry, Moulton, all of them in little rooms writing letters to each other, furiously composing, measuring out their agonies and their heart's desires. Blotted ink, crazy calligraphy, the morning post! In my dreaming they were all in one great old house, and the Giant Landlord had forbidden them to speak; so they rustled about, stuffing letters in little hiding places, a scavenger hunt of the heart—which fancy I was jolted out of by the spectre of a great dead eagle floating down to sit on my head.

Grabbing talons from my scalp, careful not to spill claret, I saw Henry walking in the winter park of barren sycamores, his freezing face thrust up close to mine, his imploring eyes. And if I had been surprised by his sudden intimacy—especially after he had opened his newspaper one morning over mackerel to discover that I had "registered my protest twenty years ago" (oh! how I dreamed the dead drumbeat of those syllables)—I saw him now, saw his intimacies with them all. And I understood why he had so suddenly trusted Francis Moulton, how he had become the helpless dependent of Von Moltke. As I saw butchers rubbing shoulders with industrialists, and shoemakers passing congress-men, in and out of the house, with stories of what Mrs. Tilton had bought here, and what Mr. Tilton had left to be mended there, the Garfield nomination, the El Dorado of California, straight facts and rude shocks, I knew that hundreds of people thought that they had known Henry Ward Beecher.

They had.

Courtroom words sprang to visionary life, there in the cradled claret glass, warming in my hand. "Possession of her person." Mother, I am a hero. Her kiss be frost. Abraham Lincoln. Henry's great public family! When Plymouth Church had celebrated its Silver Jubilee in 1872, the twenty-fifth anniversary of Henry's installation, Theodore Tilton said, "My dear Henry, you will never have such an opportunity to resign amid the world's good opinion as now. It can be known to all that you have gone to see with your own eyes the footprints of the Master whose life you are now writing." Henry had mentioned to me those words—he had not breathed a syllable of what they meant. '72, the same year Henry gave the Yale Lectures—as the first incumbent of the Lyman Beecher Lectureship on Preaching (and Father wouldn't send his young son Henry to Yale, thought him "too stupid" for New Haven). No wonder Henry finally cried out, "I would not have believed that anyone could pass through my experience and be alive or sane."

Old Bowen was having his way.

At the house on Columbia Heights that night, Henry was especially distressed—one of his favorite fireside poets, Mr. Whittier, had been quoted in the public press: "I have loved Beecher so much! I cannot believe him guilty as charged, and yet it looks very dark." Henry was so hurt, and now he was entreating Hatty, who was in charge of *belles lettres,* to intercede on his behalf. I had left them downstairs in colloquy, and repaired to my make-shift bed in a little anteroom upstairs. I lay awake for some time, thinking over the terrible deep hurt we were in, thinking that I did not understand it—the way the brain tumbles with worry. At first I thought I was dreaming, when the voices reached my ears, but gradually I roused myself, and it was Hatty and Henry still talking together, upstairs now, just on the other side of that anteroom wall. I could not safely get away, and not knowing how long they had been speaking, I held my breath.

"You wrote it to me twenty-eight years ago next month. Of course I've kept it:

Dearest Hat:

I almost always feel that my friends despise me. I know I don't deserve it—tho they think I do. I don't—for I am not deceitful. I am careless, *Oh, don't you show this to* anybody. *I don't want Father to feel bad, ever, for he is always kind to me—but I think he feels a* sorrowful *kindness and that is what* cuts *me. . . ."*

Hatty's voice trailed off into weeping.

I had to knock on the wall, but I could not. Lying there helpless in the cot.

Henry was comforting her. He was holding her, I knew he was holding her. Then they were lamenting the antic behavior of Belle, her insane blackmail scheme to get Henry to confess. Hatty's voice: "No one can understand The Woodhull's hold, the secret of her influence over our poor little sister. It is an incredible infatuation."

"And Belle is a lovely woman."

"She was—before this witch took control of her."

"In the old days we were all so happy."

Harriet: "These are things that strike my very life. Accusations against you—I cannot hear them discussed. I feel such an intense uprising, and if ever I hear those who ought to know better wandering out insinuations about you there will be—there will be an eruption of a volcano that has for years been supposed to be extinct. They'll see what I am!"

"Hat, you're the best of us all."

She was quiet. "At least now there is no fear that you will not fight."

"No. No fear."

"Your eyes are at last opened—you see Tilton in his naked depravity and barrenness."

Henry must have done something when Hatty said that, for she suddenly gave a little heartbroken laugh and spoke very rapidly: "It has been hard work to convince you, dear simple-hearted man, that such baseness and treachery exist. Oh, the process of opening your eyes—it was like dividing soul and body—but now the noble old Lion is rousing himself—"

"Wait 'til I roar."

"Oh, how weakly you have been trusted—and Tilton bringing up all the old Bowen slanders."

There it was—I pulled the blanket up around me, off my toes—the old Bowen slanders—what, what?

"Henry, I love you so much—you don't know how much—you see how it makes me cry to think of it. Oh, this love—if we could only have enough of it."

And Henry's voice, calm and comforting: "Hat, I have lived over again the years we had together—

before the plunge into matrimony first gave you, and then me, to the sea of life, and all its innumerable waves. Now we are shipwrecked sailors, on little islands, looking at each other across the waters—"

And then Cold Tom did moan, without meaning to.

In early March Theodore Tilton took the stand. Due to a late arrival of my train from Elmira (we had had to wait for a loco-motive from Albany) I contented myself with a little temporary chair some rows away in the back and far to the right; Eunice was directly in my line of eye-shot to Tilton. But even from my inferior position I could see that Eunice—who had been so impassive, so perfectly self-possessed as to be almost trance-like, her snow-white hair poised perfectly above her black woolen wrap—when Tilton took the stand I could see Eunice's clear eyes begin to—positively to—glitter.

Theodore Tilton sat like a Vice-President. In his olive waistcoat, primly buttoned; his golden locks swaying with the Byronic moves of his head. "My wife sinned as one in a trance. I don't think she was a free agent. She would have done Henry Ward Beecher's bidding if, like the heathen-priest in the Hindoo-land, he had bade her fling her child into the Ganges or cast herself under the Juggernaut."

Q: "Have you expressed violent hostility to Mr. Beecher?"
A: "I have expressed hostility."
Q: "Have you expressed violent hostility?"
A: "I have expressed hostility violently."

Behind me an elderly man was arguing with a policeman: "If I don't get in thar and get one look at Henry Ward Beecher my wife Sairy will fret and scold dreadful." I looked at Henry Ward Beecher. He was spread out in his chair, yawning, his eyes dawdling on a fresco in the dome. The heathen-priest in the Hindoo-land.

All that week we were given a cannonade of domestic letters. What astonished me was Mr. Tilton reading them, reading them aloud in the courtroom, backed by the American flag, the most intimate letters of husband and wife, declaimed to reporters:

Lib to Theo: *"Oh, how my soul yearns over you two dear men! I do love him dearly, and I do love you supremely, utterly, believe it. Perhaps, if by God's grace I keep myself white, I may bless you both. I am striving. Now, beloved, let not even the* shadow *of a shadow fall on your dear heart because of this. You once told me you did not believe that I gave you a correct account of his visits, and you always felt that I repressed much."*

Repressed much? Oh, hear the child striving to keep herself white—and why does she bother her husband with all them "ifs"?

Lib to Theo: *"I have now an inflamed eyelid and looseness of the bowels, which renders my coming to you impracticable. Adieu."*

Lib to Theo: *"Sometimes I lie awake hours because I have no arms to nestle in. Adieu. It is dreadful to be so full of feeling as I am at this moment. Again, Adieu."*

His letters to her—"In the cars, Northern Indiana," "Dubuque, Iowa," "Quincy, Illinois"—he read them with positive relish:

If you should ever appear to me anything less than the ideal woman, a Christian saint, I shall not care to live a day longer. You promised the other man to cleave to me, and yet you leave me all alone and cleave to him. O Frailty! Thy name is woman!

The two of them—children—tossed their tempests back and forth, and now her inflamed eyelid and loose bowels were public property. This woman, this little lady-child said, "Tears baptised me," and confessed, "It is a physical impossibility for me to tell the truth." Whatever it was she was telling, the fatal day was fixed after the death from cholera of their little boy, Paul. Henry preached at the funeral— Theodore had hardly known little Paul, he had been away so much. And then, on October 10,—"it" first happened, when Lib was drowning in grief, when Henry was probably drowning in tears to bathe that grief—her subpoenaed diary had the properly ambiguous entry for October 10—"A Day Memorable."

So "it" began to happen.

"it."

Henry and Lib, *Norwood* and perfumed soap and buggy rides and—and "*it*"?

Or Tilton's inflamed fancy? The *Herald* wrote, "Now Tilton stands before us, or rather, he does not stand, for that is the characteristic attitude of manhood, but squats before us, a leering obscene shape, coprophagous and foul, beslobbering with tears and self-adulation the letters of the woman he had sworn to love. It is simply horrible."

I had come to enjoy the way the ancient vendor of sandwiches haunted the courthouse, discovering his power. When one day he was told that his mince pies were bad, he said, "Werry bad, sir, but not half as bad as the langwidge you've been a listunin to."

Theodore Tilton seemed to recognize what was happening; when court resumed the following Monday he was in stiff control. He was a talking book:

"In the early part of July 1870, my wife came home unexpectedly from the country, and said to me that the object of her return was to communicate to me a secret, which had long been resting on her mind like a burden, which she wished to throw off; that she had, on several previous occasions, come almost to the point of making such a statement to me, and once in particular while on a sickbed, but that she had never until then, having been restored to health, been brought quite to the point of courage to make the disclosure; that before she would announce to me what the secret was, she exacted from me a pledge that I would do no harm to the person concerning whom the secret was to be told, and furthermore that I would not communicate to that person the fact that she had made such a revelation to me, because she wished to inform him of that revelation herself. I gave to her my pledge, my word of honor, that I would neither disclose her secret nor would I injure the person concerned. Then she said to me that it was a secret between herself and the Rev. Henry Ward Beecher, her pastor; that, as I was well aware, there had been, during a long course of years, a friendship between herself and her pastor; that this friendship, contrary to my expectation or belief, had been in later years more than friendship, it had been love; that it had been more than love, it had been sexual intimacy; that this sexual intimacy had begun shortly after the death of Paul; that she had been in a tender frame of mind, consequent upon that bereavement; that she had received much consolation from her pastor during that shadow on our house; that she had made a visit to his house while she was still suffering from that sorrow, and that there, on the tenth of October 1868, she had surrendered her body to him in sexual embrace; that she had repeated such an act on the following Saturday evening at her own residence, 174 Livingston Street; that she had consequent upon those two occasions, repeated such acts at various times, at his residence and at hers, and at other places—such acts of sexual intercourse continuing from the Fall of 1868 to the Spring of 1870."

It was a remarkable, poised account. Henry's attorney, Mr. Evarts, had been sitting on the edge of the defense counsel table; one brown tweed leg swinging absently, like that of a bashful boy on a gate. He said, "Mr. Tilton, do I understand that this is what you said to Mr. Beecher on that fateful night at Mr. Moulton's—you apprised him of this, and did not charge him with improper solicitation?"

Theodore was ready. "Precisely, sir; that she had in the early stages of their friendship been greatly distressed at rumors concerning Mr. Beecher's moral integrity; that she wished to show him that there was a woman who was superior to the silly flatteries with which many ladies in his congregation had courted his society; that she wished to demonstrate the honor and dignity of her sex; that she had done so in her own thought, until finally she had been persuaded by him, that as their love was proper and not wrong, therefore it followed that any expression of that love, whether by the shake of the hand, or the kiss of the lips, or even bodily intercourse, since it all was the expression of that which in itself was not wrong, therefore that bodily intercourse was not wrong; that she had said to me that Mr. Beecher had professed a greater love than he had ever shown to any woman in his life; that she and I both knew that for years his home had not been a happy one; that his wife had not been a satisfactory wife to him—"

Theodore did not look at Eunice Bullard Beecher—he, perhaps, could feel the heatwaves coming from those glittering eyes; but I looked at her, and she seemed only to say, Yes, we know this part, yes, go on, little boy, we shall hear it all—

"—that Mr. Beecher wished to find in her, Elizabeth, the consolation, the help to his mind, and the solace of life which had been denied to him by the unfortunate marriage at home; that he had made these arguments to her during the early years of their friendship, and she had steadfastly resisted; that he had many times fondled her to the degree that it required on her part bodily resistance to be rid of him; that after her final surrender during the period of her sorrow, in October 1868, he had then many times solicited her when she had refused, that the occasions of her yielding her body to him had not been numerous, but that his solicitations had been frequent and urgent, and sometimes violent— finally, that she felt she never could look me honestly in the face again until she had made a full and free confession; that she had come down from the country on purpose to make it."

Q: "And you told all this to Mr. Beecher as you are telling it to us now?"

A: "Yes. I told it from a little memorandum that I had made, of dates, times, extracts from letters—a little memorandum made on the back of a white envelope—and in the course of my narration to Mr. Beecher I unconsciously picked the paper to pieces."

Q: "And what did Mr. Beecher do?"

A: "He sat in his chair, and I thought he was about to speak; I waited a moment; his face and his head, and his neck, were blood-red, and I feared there would be some accident to him. He burst out: 'Theodore, I am in a dream.' I went to the door, unlocked it, and said, 'You are free to retire.' He did not seem to hear what I said; and I again pointed to the door and said that he might go. Then he suddenly looked me in the face, and said, 'May I go once again, and for the last time, to see Elizabeth?' I instantly answered no, and then, yes. 'But in going to Elizabeth, see to it, sir, that you do not chide her for her confession. She is at home—sick, heartbroken. Visit upon her no reproach, for if you smite her with a word, I will smite you in a ten-fold degree. I spared your life when I had power to destroy it; I spare it now for Elizabeth's sake; but if you reproach her, I will smite your name before all the world.' Mr. Beecher stood a moment on the threshold, and putting both his hands up to his head—the redness in his face increasing all the while—said, 'This is all a wild whirl,' and he left me and went down the stairs with his hand on the rail, staggering, and I thought he was about to fall."

Tilton sat there, resolute in olive and white. The noon recess was called, and I shook myself—fairly shook myself—at the sudden discovery that I believed every word.

We returned from luncheon
to find an auxiliary attorney, young Mr. Fullerton, in
elegantly brushed black.

Q: "Let us go on with your narrative, Mr.
   Tilton—to the next interview you had with Mr.
   Beecher. This was on or about the third of
   January?"
A: "Yes, sir."
Q: "And where did it take place?"
A: "It took place in precisely the same room in
   which the other was held, that is, the second
   story, front room, in Mr. Moulton's house in
   Clinton Street. Mr. Moulton had not yet risen,
   being slightly unwell. While I was sitting with
   him the door bell rang and suddenly, without

any expectation on my part, and I think also without any expectation on Mr. Moulton's part, Mr. Beecher entered the room. I instantly arose from my chair, and what I did I do not exactly know. I only remember that Mr. Moulton suddenly said to me that I ought not to refuse to salute Mr. Beecher in his house. I said, 'How can you expect me to speak to a man who has ruined my wife, broken my home, and who then gets my permission, in this sad hour, to visit that woman, and uses that permission for the purpose of dictating to her and making her write down a lie?' Mr. Moulton then said to me, 'But Theodore, you must remember that Mr. Beecher has sent to you a letter through me humbling himself before you as he does before God. What more can you ask of him? What more could you ask of any man in such circumstances? Furthermore,' said he, 'this is my house, and Mr. Beecher is present as my guest, and you will oblige me if you speak to him, at least as much as to say, good morning.' I did say, 'Mr. Beecher, good morning.' Mr. Beecher meanwhile sat on the edge of Mr. Moulton's bed. He turned around to me and said, 'Theodore, I don't marvel that you do not feel like speaking to me. I feel more dread of being spoken to by you than you can possibly feel repugnance. All I have to say is that I hope you found it in your heart to accept my letter— I dictated it out of heartbreak and anguish. It expressed my sincere feelings. Nevertheless,' said he, 'I know it was but words, and words are little and nothing, and no words of mine can ever undo the great wrong that I have done to you and to Elizabeth. I will bow my head and go out of public life. I have only one request to make—that if it be necessary for you to make a public recital of this case, that you will give me notice in advance, so that I may either go out of the world by suicide, or else escape from the face of my friends by a voyage to some foreign land.' He added, 'Your wife was not to blame.' And this he repeated two or three times over—'The blame belonged to me and not to her.' Tears came to his eyes and he said, 'Tell me, can you possibly ever reinstate Elizabeth in your respect and love?' He then buried his face in his hands; he sat near the foot of Mr. Moulton's bed. He said that he was dizzy. He said he was in great grief through Mr. Bowen's action in my case, the termination of my engagements with Mr. Bowen's newspapers, and he felt that Mr. Bowen had cashiered me because of statements that he himself had made. Whereupon he was led into another violent outburst of grief. He sat and wept, again and again, and his face assumed a very peculiar redness, in the midst of which Mr. Moulton asked me if I would retire and leave the two together alone. Which I did."

The packed courtroom was still as death, except this was life, life of the most serious and dramatic texture—our life, as real as novels—and Theodore Tilton's grasp of it was complete.

Not until a voice spoke from the back of the courtroom and we turned to see Mr. Evarts, did we remember that he must have been listening for some time. "If it please the court," he said, striding forward, "I now move to raise the question that formed a considerable element in our discussions of last week in Your Honor's chambers, and which I do not propose to renew at any length. I move to strike out the evidence given of this interview. It is evidence upon the part of the husband with the purpose to disparage the reputation of the wife, to wit, to prove her adultery. Of course it does not prove it. It is merely a statement of what passed between him and Mr. Beecher, as based upon something that may or may not have passed between him and his wife. Your Honor has not allowed that to be proved as a matter of fact. I therefore move to strike the testimony out, it not being competent by our laws for the husband or the wife to testify against the repute of another in that degree of crimination."

The Judge, knowing an old familiar story, denied the motion.

Mr. Evarts said, "Must I take an exception, sir?"

The Judge said, "Exception is noted."

Mr. Evarts seemed to know the story as well as the Judge, for when Mr. Fullerton sat down, Evarts approached the witness, and startled not only him but also the rest of us; he said, "Sir, did you ever say Victoria Woodhull was crazy?"

Theodore colored. "Crazy?"

Q: "Come now, Mr. Tilton, you said she was crazy."

A: "I am not sure just what—oh, I have you, Mr. Evarts—yes, I said she was crazy. Like Joan of Arc or Swedenborg."

Q: "An Enthusiast?"

A: "Well—a rapt idealist."

Q: "And you became her pupil?"

A: "Not exactly, sir. Not her pupil."

Q: "In what capacity did you—did you serve her?"
A: "Serve, sir?"
Q: "Well, did you ever play chess with Elizabeth Cady Stanton?"
A: "Yes."
Q: "Did you ever appear undressed in Susan B. Anthony's?"
A: "No, sir, and I cannot imagine any reasons why anyone should."

The court restored order.

Q: "You have not associated with public women?"
A: "Never."
Q: "I don't mean prostitutes, I mean reformers."
A: "Oh—" Mr. Tilton, his face caught off guard, was again the object of merriment.

Mr. Evarts turned to quiet the audience; then he faced the jury box, where some of the gentlemen had appreciated the by-play, the foreman leaning eagerly on his ebony cane. Mr. Evarts said, "That Theodore Tilton went down to Coney Island with Victoria Woodhull in a carriage is admitted by him. He denies that he went bathing with her. We shall satisfy you, gentlemen, that he is mistaken; that when they arrived at Coney Island they deposited their watches in the custody of the coachman, and they went to the sea shore, as if to bathe—all, of course, for the sake of Mr. Beecher, and to preserve him from this scandalous publication. And we shall show you that when they returned, the golden locks of Mr. Tilton were damp with the mists of the ocean, at least, or perhaps he will say that they were dampened by the perspiration that he suffered on account of the agony that he was enduring for the sake of Henry Ward Beecher. We shall show you that they returned to the carriage with all the evidences that they had been bathing together. We shall show you that when he drove them back to this city, the coachman stopped at the house of Frank Moulton, and late in the evening they ordered a covered carriage and Mr. Tilton went home with Mrs. Woodhull. We shall show you that he discharged the carriage at that house, and the coachman left him there, where, we suppose, he remained all night—earnestly arguing to save the skin of Henry Ward Beecher." Mr. Evarts changed his tone. With great earnestness he now said, "Theodore Tilton stimulated this woman to the publication of this scandal rather than to its suppression. And we shall show you that the remarks he attributes to Henry Ward Beecher—that 'marriage is the grave of love,' that 'bodily intercourse is based on love rather than lust,' that 'sexual embrace is as natural an expression of love as the shake of the hand or the kiss of the lips'—that these, gentlemen, are not the words of the Pastor of Plymouth Church—they are the seditious and demented proclamations of the *Spirituelle* of Free Love!"

The audience, not knowing whether to clap for the rhetorical effort or to hiss the female, hooted and applauded with equal intensity.

"But first, Mr. Tilton, I should like to question you on your—literary productions. Are you the author of *Sir Marmaduke's Musings?*"

Tilton, controlling himself, nodded.

"And did you publish to the world, in 1872, when rumors of this scandal were rife, did you publish that poem of which I may read a fragment?—

> I clasped a woman's breast,
> As if her heart I knew,

Or fancied, would be true,
Who proved—alas, she too!—
False like the rest."

Tilton sat there.

Judge Neilson leaned over. "The witness will answer the question."

Tilton's face bolted, but he played with his midriff button. "Yes, I am the author of those lines."

"And did Mr. Beecher speak to you about them?"

"Yes, he said he thought they were—unwise."

"That you published them?"

"His criticism was not of a literary nature, sir."

"He thought the poem was a defamation of Elizabeth, did he not?"

Tilton had not prepared a script. He leaned forward, furious and cool. "Sir?"

"You composed that poem with a revolver on the table? The poem was a suicide note?"

"I don't believe, sir, and you know—I—"

"No mind, no mind." Evarts turned another page in his dossier. "This one—'*Aimer, aimer, c'est a vivre!*' Is this one yours?"

"My errors in French have been called to my—"

But Mr. Evarts swiftly went to the poem, reading it all, each stanza provoking mirth in the audience as Evarts threw his wondrous capacity into baroque parody:

"French is always spoken best
Breathing deeply from the chest—
Darling, does your bosom heave?
Aimer, aimer, c'est a vivre!

He calmed his lava, and then erupted again:

> Or, if I presume too much,
> Teaching French by sense of touch,
> Grant me pardon and reprieve!
> *Aimer, aimer, c'est a vivre!*

When he had murdered the last stanza the laughter in the courtroom was uproarious. It could not be controlled, it could not.

Until a hush fell over us, for "The Woodhull" had appeared. A great gasp went up from the gallery, and we turned to see our national enchantress standing there, in a pale blue beaded gown, the tea-rose at her throat. She offered to the court a packet of materials ribboned in scarlet. A recess was called so that counsel could have opportunity to examine. I groaned—more letters! The Plymouth party vociferously denounced the sudden presence of the wicked witch, but she was the delight of the reporters, standing in the great echoing hallway, her voice alert and full of quick mischief. Yes, said she, she had written to Theodore Tilton, "I see a coffin following you out to Cincinnati," when the Republican convention was held there, when it nominated Horace Greeley, who did indeed die at the end of November—another of Victoria's prophecies fulfilled. "Yes," she said to a young reporter from the *Argus*, "I conceive that Mrs. Tilton's love for Mr. Beecher was her true marriage and that her marriage to Mr. Tilton was prostitution." I was hanging on to frail, shaking Catharine, afraid that she would go after Victoria with a hat-pin.

"Yes," said The Woodhull, "after the *Weekly*

exposed the hypocrisy, Mr. Tilton came to me, and asked me who the 'eminent public teacher' might be. I said, 'I refer, sir, to the Rev. Henry Ward Beecher and your wife. And I can read, sir, by the expression on your face, that my charge is true."

A man from the *Sentinel* wondered if Theodore had joined The Women on the spot.

"Theodore said to me, 'There is one thing that I was born for, and that is war. I shall be the Samson who will destroy the temple—I will pull down the pillars of the temple, and although Mr. Beecher and my family are crushed, I shall be crushed with them.' "

Everyone around us was furiously scribbling. There were some hoots in the back, mainly from women, but one gentleman kept waving his umbrella, like relevance, in the air.

Theodore Tilton himself, with an ample bodyguard of attorneys, passed amongst us.

A reporter called out, "Mrs. Woodhull, what do you think of Mr. Tilton now?"

Theodore stopped, as if mistaking the direction of the question, as if it were put to him.

Victoria's eyes looped through the crowd to settle against his. She was silent for a moment, and then: "I think his attempt to implicate Mr. Beecher is a little schoolboy's sniveling—'He made me do it, if it hadn't been for him, I shouldn't have done it.' He is a laughingstock. I have said before that I believe Mr. Tilton will make quite a man if he should live to grow up."

At which Theodore slank out with his phalanx. And better so. Much better so—Victoria Woodhull continued her amazing performance. Had she been bathing with Tilton at Coney Island? She proclaimed, the reporters took it all down, "I ought to know Mr. Tilton, for he was my devoted lover for more than half a year. So enamored and infatuated were we with each other that for three months we were hardly out of each other's sights and he slept every night in my arms."

That was enough for Catharine, who went off with Hatty in search of some female relief. I was glad I stayed until The Woodhull was quite done, for in close conversation with a cub from Cleveland, she gave Henry Ward Beecher a score of "Amativeness 8."

In the cafe, I gobbled kippers and enjoyed my beer.

With the concurrence of both sides, the Woodhull's letters were not to be introduced as evidence.

Mr. Evarts was clearly eager to detonate his final torpedoes. "If Mr. Tilton could realize the sad truth that he is morally dead, he would still rejoice in this post-mortem investigation of his character. But we propose to dissect him first in the interest of truth and bury him afterward in the interest of decency." He turned. "Mr. Tilton, did your wife write to you that your loss of faith had nullified your marriage?"

Tilton objected to the formation of the question, but before he could finish the nature of his objection, Mr. Evarts had asked, "In one of your letters did you call yourself a 'hypocrite, a deceiver, a whited sepulchre filled with dead man's bones'?"

Tilton unbuttoned his coat. "The tongue is a wild beast that no man can tame."

"Were you referring to the Winsted scandal— the daughter of—of a Congressman in Winsted, Connecticut, the seventeen-year-old girl whom you debauched before—"

Counsel for the plaintiff rose—Mr. Pryor and

Mr. Fullerton both—and Mr. Evarts withdrew the question. He quickly again put in another, "Did you call the radical feminists 'human hyenas'? Did you call them 'a holocaust of womanhood'?"

"I'm not sure—I—"

Q: "Why, Mr. Tilton, are you never certain?"

A: "But you asked me if I was *sure*."

Q: "Oh, I beg your pardon, Mr. Tilton, I had not realized there was that wide a difference between sure and certain."

A: "Mr. Evarts, I am *certain* that the sun rose yesterday, but I am *sure* it will rise tomorrow."

Q: "That is the distinction?"

A: "Yes."

Q: "Are you sure about it, or certain?"

Tilton hated the laughter.

Q: "Well, tell me this—did you ever say the *surest* way of securing Mr. Beecher's aid was to accuse him of having wronged you? Once convince him that he has done you an injury, and there is nothing you can ask that he will not do."

Theodore Tilton could not admit it, but he could not deny it.

"Mr. Tilton, did you not testify that you said to Mr. Beecher, when you were brought together at Moulton's—did you not say to him, 'Writing that letter demanding that you leave Brooklyn was a grand thing to do, but it would have been grander not to have done it'?"

Tilton nodded, and then blushed absolutely scarlet when Evarts implored the heavens: "Oh, what a happy condition a man is in when whatever he does is grand, and if he hadn't done it, it would have been grander!"

The audience adored it, and had to be silenced again.

"Did you not testify that at the time of Plymouth's Silver Jubilee, Mr. Beecher said to you, 'When men are at the point of their prosperity, they are sometimes nearest to their downfall'? Was it not then that you saw your way clear—when you told him to go to the Holy Land, to finish his *Life of Christ?* Did you not think, well, people will say to themselves, where there's smoke, there's fire? Where there is so much smoke there must be some fire—if the story is not true, something must be true?"

At the plaintiff's table Mr. Pryor stood up and gave a brief speech about the impropriety of Mr. Evarts' line of questioning.

So Mr. Evarts was pure and simple: "Why—why, Mr. Tilton, did you keep this secret so closely guarded, for all these long years, before bringing it to public court?"

Tilton, neither sure nor certain: "I—I thought I could bear it all alone. I would never tell. For a period of weeks I lived in a kind of ecstasy. I walked the streets as if I scarcely touched the ground, and the greatness of the temptation I had put away, the magnanimity of the life I was leading, the sacrifice—it made me radiant, so that I wrote without labor."

"You *wrote?*"

"Yes, sir."

"Then why did you break your—ecstasy of concealment?"

A cloud passed over Theodore Tilton's face, and

he articulated the lightning in it: "To have Mr. Beecher creep like a snake into my house, leaving his pollution behind him, and I so blind as not to see, and esteeming him all the while as a saint. Oh, it is too much!"

Thomas Kinnicut Beecher had one of his frequent little prickings of disloyalty: by God, the man is right, he may be a fool and a blackguard, but the misery of the man is real, and the wrong done to him is clear.

"We have just been honored by an unexpected visit from Victoria Woodhull, so perhaps, Mr. Tilton, you could tell us a little more about how you came to write her campaign biography."

"She"—Theodore was trying desperately to regain his composure after that sight of her in the hall at recess, surrounded by reporters—"she—she sent for me. She put into my hands a roll of manuscript that she said was a biographical sketch of her life, written by her husband; it was not written as satisfactorily as she desired it to be; and she asked me if I—if I would take it and read it, and revise it, or amend it, to make it out anew. She wanted it more readily to command the popular ear. So I—I took that manuscript and—I read it, I read it twice—and instead of merely revising it, I sat down, and at one heat I wrote the sum and substance. After it was done I took it to her house in the evening. I read it to her. I had done it as well as I could. She expressed great dissatisfaction with it. She said to me, 'You have left out the most important parts.' And I said, 'Well, I have left out some extravagant parts that I thought would mar the narrative.'"

"You are a thoughtful man."

"But she said, 'I wish you would put them in

again.' I said, 'What? Do you want me to say that you have called a dead child to life?' 'Yes,' said she, 'I do. To write my life and leave out that incident would be to play the part of Hamlet with Hamlet omitted.' I said, 'Do you want me to say that you have had the power to heal the sick, like the apostles?' 'Yes,' said she, 'I do, because it is the exact truth.' And I asked her if she wanted me to say also that she had communication from the spirit world from the Greek orator Demosthenes; and she said, 'Yes, for sometimes he speaks through me.' 'Very well,' said I, 'if you want them all in I will put them in.' So I took that manuscript, which I thought I had completed, and I sat at the writing-table in her third room, her back parlor—it was a summer night—and I spent hours writing in those supplemental incidents. I was until two or three o'clock in the morning. I completed the manuscript. When it was done I threw myself down on the sofa and slept."

Theodore Tilton was still—writing. Mr. Evarts had backed away, had sat down at the defense table, and was enjoying the spectacle with the rest of us. On the witness stand Tilton was in a world of his own, the world of his literary sensibility, lost in the Gothic narrative of his life where trees split open in storms and the long grasses conceal pheasants from the deluge—a spectacle such as I had never seen before, a man disappearing into his own novel:

"And then—and then a few weeks after that, possibly six or seven, Mr. Moulton told me that he had received from Mr. Beecher a letter that Victoria had written to him, asking that he might preside at a public meeting in Steinway Hall, and I went the next day to Mr. Moulton's house on purpose to be present at an interview appointed to be held among

Mrs. Woodhull, Mr. Beecher, and Mr. Moulton. I reached the house too late. Mrs. Woodhull had been there and had gone. Mr. Beecher was there, and Mr. Moulton was there. They told me the result of the interview. Mrs. Woodhull had urged him to preside at her lecture, and he had made objections to doing so. I told him that I thought he should preside. I told him that I had once presided at a lecture for her. And, by the way, in my narrative I have omitted to state that one evening I presided for her at Cooper Institute when she delivered a lecture on Finance"—Theodore Tilton suddenly awakened from his novel to the scene in the hallway that noon, and his eyes came unfocused—"it was a perfectly harmless and stupid production of which I think nobody has heard since"—and then he lapsed again, back into the gorgeous stream of his own endeavors: "I said, 'I have once presided for Mrs. Woodhull; nothing came of it; no harm grew out of it, and if you, Mr. Beecher, will go and preside at her meeting you can do it without harm to yourself, and you will put her in that public way under such obligation to you that I think she has been put under to me. I don't think that woman can ever injure me after what I have—after what I have done for her' "—and now Mr. Tilton was truly awake, he saw that he was not writing a novel, he was digging a grave—

Mr. Evarts said, "Do continue, sir; we are enthralled."

"I—I only said to Mr. Beecher that she would consider it an act of courtesy, and—and it will be a new bond, a bond by which we shall all be able to hold her against any—any ebullition of her strange mind. But he refused. When the night arrived, a great crowd was present. Mr. Moulton said, 'Why, we can't get in.' I replied, 'There are more doors than one to Steinway Hall, I have been here before; there is a rear entrance, and I—I—'"

"Yes."

"Victoria speaks best when hissed at. The crowd was unruly. I found her backstage, full of fire. She said, 'Whenever I find a social carbuncle I shall plunge my surgical knife of reform into it, up to the hilt.' She was to speak on—sexual slavery."

"Well, we are all of us certainly plunged into that."

The courtroom was restlessly gleeful.

"Victoria Woodhull has been arrested eight times, spent weeks in jail—all at the bidding of Mr. Beecher's minions—"

The restless glee turned to shouting.

"And can I add that I had hoped this trial could be conducted throughout with that quietness and that decorum that should always characterize proceedings in a court of justice—whatever may take place in a Church in the City of Brooklyn!"

Astonishment! Now the courtroom was a mob! Judge Neilson addressed the sergeant of police—requesting additional officers. The sergeant said that he had already made two or three arrests. The Judge told him to try a dozen.

In the hub-bub Mr. Evarts decided to strike. He closed Mr. Tilton's narrative with a question: "Now are you aware that Mrs. Woodhull had written to Henry Ward Beecher: 'Two of your sisters have gone out of the way to assail my character, both by means of the public press. You doubtless know that it is within my power to strike back, but I do not desire to do this. I speak guardedly, but I think you will understand me.' Do you admit to an awareness of this letter?"

Tilton nodded.

"Then you are also—"

"Excuse me, sir," Tilton interrupted, "I do believe you have left out the most interesting part—where Victoria says Mr. Beecher told her that every time he married a couple he felt 'condemned'—he told her that if he were to preach her doctrines he should preach to empty seats and it would be the ruin of his Church."

"Oh, that *is* an interesting part."

"I only meant—"

"Yes, we know."

"But sir, you are twisting—"

"Sir, *you* are twisting."

"Mr. Evarts, the plain facts—"

"The plain fact of the Steinway Hall address was its title: 'Free Love, Marriage, Divorce, and Prostitution.'"

"Yes."

"And you wanted Henry Ward Beecher to preside? You induced him, with threats, to preside. You compelled him to preside. But he would not. You had to get him connected with her. But you couldn't. Is that not the plain fact, sir?"

Tilton turned to the Judge, who turned away. And then Theodore Tilton rambled into a discourse of such turbulence that the whole courtroom had suddenly sunk underwater, and bright fleeting things were being glimpsed in a liquid coral. Tilton talked about the "plain fact—the *plain fact*" he kept repeating, of "*the paternity of Ralph*," their ten-year-old son, Theodore Tilton was saying that he had long suspected that Mr. Beecher—he had dates, memoranda—"*the paternity of Ralph*"—no man knows—he looks suddenly into his son's eyes, for a shade of his own, and to see there the haunting glimmer of another man, to read in a child's eyes the sudden destruction of every decency, every compact, every holiest covenant—and he had wanted to keep that secret, keep it buried, never to let the boy know—though now the boy would bear the blot of his uncertain paternity throughout his life—he could no longer save it—the paternity of the boy Ralph— little Ralph, who used to hold his toes up to the fire to be named—it was over now, all over, all doomed, there is no light in the world, the light has gone out, with the paternity of the boy Ralph—and only a minister—only a minister, in this fallen and moribund age, could distinguish between a consecration and a sacrament, a true minister, a minister of holiness—

Mr. Evarts, in the silence that held the courtroom spellbound, whispered, "You are not a minister, Mr. Tilton?"

"No, sir—no sir! It is the single distinction I possess. Thank *God* I am not a minister! No—no—I want you to put that down, Mr. Stenographer. I despise the Church. I *despise* the *Church*. I saw the cowardice of the Church in the great anti-slavery fight, and it has always been false. I do not believe—I do not believe in one of the thirty-nine articles. I do not believe in either of the catechisms, I do not believe in the divine inspiration of Scriptures, I do not believe in the divinity of Christ, I do not believe—"

"THEODORE!" A blast of agony and despair— immediately asserted, no sooner asserted than contradicted—a volcano of pain in one word—and it had been uttered by Henry Ward Beecher, in the audience, Henry Ward Beecher standing up in his loose black coat, his ragged hair in a mess, his hands out like webby gloves, his face—anguish incarnate!—a garish fixture in a dream, a man in Brooklyn Court—now looking to this brimming, boiling man of the golden locks—Henry Ward Beecher's body, capable of criminal possession, capable of the paternity of the boy Ralph, all of Henry up now, erect, and forcefully tipping forward at the spectacle of Tilton ruining himself—"I *despise* the *Church*"—and pleasure passed over Henry's face, quick and ghastly, running for cover in the abundance of pain—

THEODORE!

I lunched with Dr. John T. Wood, who had directed the excavations of the Temple of Diana in Asia Minor. He seemed pleased with a preacher, in this Temperance Age, who drinks a second glass of beer. "Jack" Wood was telling me of an earlier excavation at Pompeii, the memory of that coming to him through his own glass of beer, as he pondered the miracle of the morning's revelations. He was describing, I at first thought, old Tom Jefferson's characterization of a man holding a wolf by the ears, neither safe to hold on or let go. But Jack Wood had a rather different image in his mind—a little statue unearthed by a 'prentice archeologist. A small statue, Tom—terra-cotta— barely six inches high. A figure of a man with his, begging your pardon, Rev. Tom, his *grandissimus,* his enormously elongated member turning back up upon him, the head of it transformed into the head of a wolf, its jaws distended, Tom, the statue's left arm was coming round, a knife in its hand—should he kill the wolf ready to deliver the death-bite?, for in doing so he would cut off his own pego—

Said Jack Wood, "It's Theodore Tilton, Tom."

"No," I opined, "it's the old story of life—the oldest. Damned if you do, damned if you don't."

Dr. John T. Wood smiled, declared me a capital fellow, a capital fellow, Tom, and joined me on the night train for Elmira. He had heard of some artifacts currently in possession of Cornell University, a collection of figures from the Temple of Zeus.

Hatty brought Henry flowers from Roxana's grave. Henry's eyes filled, and he said, choked with the little bouquet, "Love never dies. My mother's grave blossoms for me."

I stood watching them both, and I was suddenly overcome with sadness; something about this whole great trial kept nudging me toward a large and simple lesson, one that I did not want to learn:

I'm losing him. I am losing my brother Henry. The furious engines of life, as relentless as slow time, will exact their price. And the price is bankruptcy. Even Beechers can lose each other. My Henry—"my" Henry—will always exist, will be there forever, in my head, but something is gradually tearing loose, below decks of our Beecher Boat; even if the ship makes it safely to harbor, the crew will go their separate ways. Perhaps, though, I was merely in the grip of resentment, for I had planned somehow on being more than a third mate. I was fearful that Thomas Kinnicut Beecher was the man who had kept the log and mistaken it for the voyage.

Tom jumped ship. And waited, actually, waited quietly, saying good-bye. I told my soul not to bid Hatty farewell, and stood there helplessly watching my soul do exactly that. I was swimming back to the time Hatty married Calvin, Calvin Stowe, who looked to me then as he looks to me now—like a German professor, opinionated in poor clothes, with a red nose. When their wedding day came, Hatty saw me standing around stupid, I was only a boy wearing Sunday clothes on a weekday, and Hatty took me into her room. She said, "About half an hour more, and your sly big sister will cease to be Hatty Beecher and change into nobody knows who. Do you wish to know how I feel? Well, Tom, I have been dreading and dreading the time, and lying awake all last week wondering how I should live through this overwhelming crisis, and lo! it has come, and I feel—I feel *nothing at all.*"

Right there I knew I didn't understand women—I would never understand women. Their tears are beyond me, their tears so splendidly their own. Why did Hatty marry him?—only to please Father? Calvin had already buried one wife, and since his earliest childhood in Natick he had been obsessed with—oh, I don't know what you would call them—obsessed with "visitants." It was years before he realized that they weren't people. Their quiet music and whispering make his wide little frame shake with emotion. They come through walls, erupt slowly out of curtains and chairs; in verdant landscapes and lavender weeds they enact masques, colloquies. Indians playing viols, shepherds with ivory flutes, a woman dancing, followed by a hopping dwarf. They represent nobody living or dead, but sometimes those he hates will appear in beautiful forms, and those he loves will be torn, horribly mutilated in lengthy tunnels of fog. One morning he awakened to find in his bed a blue skeleton. It disturbed him a great deal.

And Hatty married him. Hatty, a little bit of a woman, about as thin and dry as a pinch of snuff, never much to look at in her best days and now looking like a used-up article. She married a man rich in Greek, Hebrew, Latin, Arabic, and alas! in nothing else. Calvin Stowe, Hatty's poor rabbi, her poor old rab. He had read her speeches in Glasgow in '53, when *Uncle Tom* was selling three thousand copies a day, and afterwards he collected, and labelled, and stored the gold bracelets and broken shackles the people would bring to the stage. But real people fade into ghosts, and visitants become real. One day, Hatty told me, she missed her train, returned to the house, and Calvin didn't move or speak; she sat at the window; after a half an hour he said, "Oh, my dear, I thought you were one of *them*."

She is beginning to look it. All through the trial she has been preoccupied with hazy errands. An other-wordly greyness and sorrow. "Thought," she says, "intense, emotional thought, has been my disease. All that is enthusiastic, all that is impassioned in admiration and devotion, I have felt with an all-absorbing vehemence—till now I sink into deadness. Half my time, Tom, I am scarcely alive, and for the rest I am the slave of unreasonable feeling." So she brings flowers from Roxana's grave.

Calvin decided to repair a cracked pane of glass

in Eunice's kitchen window. He went to the store, came up with penny-cut sheets of tin and a little Lavoro hammer; he broke all the other panes in the window and retired upstairs in a delirium of despair.

Good-bye. Good-bye, my darlings. Old Enthusius and dearest Hatty.

Henry and Eunice lead the parade to the courtroom, Henry like a prosperous farmer, carrying his broad-brimmed hat—Eunice on his arm. Now it is months! "The Griffin" gives no sign, absolutely none, an enigma—enduring this brutal and terrible penalty of living a public life. Henry himself remains true to that creed he articulated to me back in January— he will not break! Tiltons break. Henry seems almost to enjoy it—so attentive to the sparring in the courtroom. Not exactly lucid, but marvellously impressive.

There is one issue here: stamina.

What women got and men honor.

James Woodley, a former slave, had been a servant at The Woodhull's. On the witness chair he said that Theodore Tilton had been a "ever-day" visitor at The Woodhull's place on Murray Hill; James Woodley had seen Marse Tilton and Missy Woodhull sittin' together, talkin' with arms 'round each other. When Mr. Evarts asked him if he thought there had been anything strange about that, James Woodley rolled his eyes like the house nigger he was paid to be, said he had started calkerlatin' long that line, 'specially when he saw Missy Woodhull in her nightgown and Marse Tilton standin' there in his stockin' feet, but then he knew it was all right normal cause he'd been 'splained *Free* Love.

Lots of Christian folk laughed at James Wood-ley.

Another servant from the Tilton household was called, one Catharine Carey. She said she had seen Lib sitting on Henry's lap; she had heard Mr. Beecher ask, "How do you feel, Elizabeth dear?" Lib replied, "Dear father, I feel so-so." Catharine Carey said she had been suffering from "brownkeetoes" (bronchitis); only under cross-examination did it come clear that her name was Catharine Carey *Smith,* and that her residence was now Bellevue. Tilton's attorneys had been raiding the madhouse! Mrs. Carey-Smith was asked if she had ever been discharged for "Intemperance." "No," she replied, "it wuz always intoxication." The courtroom went up again in gales of laughter.

It is the abolition of privacy.

Our most valuable witness was another house-keeper of the Tiltons', Miss Bessie Turner. The plaintiff had already charged that Henry Ward Beecher had secreted her out of town, and paid all her bills at a boarding school; she had, like so many others, "retracted" her original letter of blame:

The story that Mr. Tilton once lifted me from my bed, and carried me screaming, into his own, and attempted to violate my person, is a wicked lie.

So Mr. Evarts, dressed now in a less severe suit than his familiar brown tweed, now paying his respects to the springtime in robin's-egg blue, with a massive gold watch chain dangling in front of his vest, Mr. Evarts pointed out to her that in her original statement she had made no mention of screaming or violence—he wondered if it were not Theodore Tilton, instead of Mr. Beecher, who had had her sent away. He quoted a letter from Moulton: "She ought to be got out of town, but Theodore cannot afford to pay the expenses." Evarts played with that watch chain: "There you have it. You do not pay your neighbor's hack bill."

To clear it up once and for all, he turned to Miss Turner, a handsome woman, on a large frame, with a remarkable purple and pink hat like a melon salad with grape clusters. Mr. Evarts asked the hat why the original letter had been retracted. Bessie said, "Because I loved Mrs. Tilton, because she said if I would put my name to that paper, I would get Mr. Tilton out of all his difficulties with Henry Bowen—"

Mr. Evarts was astonished. "Henry Bowen? You mean Henry Beecher?"

"No, sir; I mean Henry Bowen. Mrs. Tilton told me that the story had got to Mr. Bowen's ears, and that all was needed was my signature."

The poor plaintiff—Miss Turner had, unawares, injected into the case the very evidence as to the purpose of manufacturing letters that the defense had been using their best arts to develop. It was Bowen, Old Bowen all the time.

Why?

"Now tell me, Miss Turner, did you notice any peculiarities in Mr. Tilton's behavior with his family?"

"Well, sir, one of his children refused meat, she did not wish for meat; Mr. Tilton looked very angry at her, and said it was all her mother's damned orthodoxy."

Laughter from the gallery.

"And did Mr. Tilton criticise anything about his wife?"

"Her grammar and her height."

Again laughter. It would make a great headline. (And it did, in the *Argus*.)

"Miss Turner, you have mentioned a habit of Mr. Tilton in regard to his being out of his room at night. Was there any particular occasion on which he visited your room at night?"

"Yes, sir. In 1867, I think it was. I had gone to bed in the second-story bedroom, front, off the sitting-room, connected by folding doors. I had not been in bed very long before Mr. Tilton came in and said he had come to kiss me good-night. I was lying on the side of the bed next the door. He went round on the other side and leaned over the bed and kissed me good-night, and he—do you want me, sir, to give all the conversation?" She looked up, concerned, as if afraid the grapes was going to fall off her hat.

Evarts told her to tell it all, and she did: "He stroked my forehead and my hair, and said what nice soft hair I had, and how nice and soft my flesh was—and then he put his hand—he was putting his hand in my neck, and I took his hand out. He says, 'Why, Bessie, my dear, you are painfully modest.' He says, 'Why, those caresses, those are all right. People in the best society do all those things, and it is perfectly proper. Nobody but people that has impure minds think of such things as that as not being right.' And I said, says I, that I could not help what they did in the best class of society. I had my own ideas of what was proper, and what was modest, and I was going to carry them out. If I didn't think it was proper for him to put his hand in my neck, I was not going to let him do it. He then laid down. He asked me if I did not—if I would not like to be married. Why, I asked him, what in the world put that into your head? Well, he said, I was an affectionate and nice girl, and I ought to be married; I ought to have a good husband. I said that I supposed when the time came—the right man came along—perhaps I would get married. But I didn't think getting married was the chief end and aim in life. It didn't trouble me very much, and that if I ever was married, there was one thing very sure, I didn't think I would ever have a *literary* man for a husband!"

The laughter and applause burst out so forcefully that Judge Neilson had to bang his gavel repeatedly, and said, "Will the officers please keep order in this audience instead of standing there idle?"

Mr. Evarts, relishing this delicious morsel, eyeing those grapes, said, "And then what, my dear?"

"Well, Mr. Tilton asked me if I didn't think some people had affinities for each other. I asked him what he meant by that—'affinities'—and he said that when a man saw a woman that he loved she should be his affinity and they live together, and that if I would allow him to caress me and love me, no harm should come to me—and that a physical expression of love was just the same as a kiss or a pat."

Evarts waved his light blue sleeves to us all: "Once again the language Mr. Tilton has attributed to Henry Ward Beecher is his own—or out on loan from The Woodhull Library."

Bessie steadying her hat, Bessie in her moment: "Oh, he told me *heaps* of ministers caressed girls and married women—it was all right and proper and beautiful. And then he told me that I was a very strange child. He says, 'Bessie, you have some very singular ideas,' and kissed me, and left."

"But he was not done with you?"

"Oh, no, sir. Another night—just after Mr. Horace Greeley had been with us, it always got Mr. Tilton excited to see Mr. Greeley—I was gone to bed and was awakened from my sleep by seeing the figure of a man standing over me, and I jumped, and I said, 'Who is there?'"

A voice from the gallery said, "God save us—not Greeley too!"

Judge Neilson sent an officer up.

Bessie Turner arranged herself on the stand; her fingers demurely frolicked with her wonderful black hair, pushing some of it up under the ripe hat. "Mr. Tilton said, 'Hush, it is only me.' And then I think I raised myself up, and I—it seemed as if I was in a strange place, all whirled around, because I had gone to bed in the second-story back bedroom, and now I was in the bedroom next to his, and I says, 'What do you—what did you bring me here for, what are you doing?' And he said that he felt lonely, he and Mr. Greeley had quarrelled, and now he wanted somebody to love him. I said, 'You would not have done this if Mrs. Tilton had been home, you should not take liberties when Mrs. Tilton is away.' But the next morning at breakfast, she did come back, with her friend Mrs. Dennis, and Mr. Tilton was very polite to her at the table, 'My dear wifey, won't you have a bit of this?' or, 'Wifey, love, won't you have a bit of that?' and she was crying so hard she could barely answer him, the tears were running down in her plate, and she excused herself and got up from the table and went into the front parlor and sat down and played some plaintive little air on the piano. After she had left the table, Mrs. Dennis said, 'What a strange woman Elizabeth is! What's she crying about? Anyone that has such a devoted husband, a nice home, and everything heart could wish for—I think she is a very singular woman.' Mr. Tilton never made her an answer, but he leaned his face on his hand, and said to me, 'Bessie, don't you think Elizabeth is demented? Don't you think she acts like a crazy woman?' Said I—and I looked at him steady in the eye—said I, 'No, I don't, but I do wonder that you haven't driven her into the lunatic asylum years ago!'"

Applause!

Mr. Evarts: "And then?"

"Well, they went—Mr. Tilton and Mrs. Tilton— they waited until Mrs. Dennis had gone, and then they went into the back parlor. I stood at the folding doors, they was open just a crack, and I saw Mr. Tilton right over near Mrs. Tilton with his fist going this way"—Bessie Turner waved her own good-sized hand, her thumb enclosed in those large fingers— "and they were talking, and he was most angry, and it was about me, what I had said, and I heard him telling her, 'You have brought that girl on to use against me, and damn it, she shall leave this house.' I opened the door and I rushed in. Said I, 'Theodore Tilton, this is not the first time I have heard you swearing at your wife, and you shall not damn her for my sake.' He said, 'Leave the room!' I said, says I, 'I won't leave the room.' Said he, 'Damn you, leave the room.' Said I, 'I won't leave the room, I will stand by Mrs. Tilton.' Then he gave me a terrible blow that hurled me the opposite side of the room, and I fell, striking my head against the door. He came forward, perfectly bland—you would think nothing in the world had ever happened—so composed and so calm—" Here Miss Turner did a splendid little imitation of her employer: she placed her hands under the armholes of an imaginary vest, and bowing her whole form forward from the witness stand, she exclaimed, " 'Why, Bessie, my dear, you tripped and fell, didn't you?' I turned around to him; said I, 'Theodore Tilton, are you a fool, or do you take me for one?' Says he, 'The God of battles is in me.' "

"And then?"

"Oh, sir, then he says he knew I had seen him stalking about the house and yelling at Mrs. Tilton for not being economical. He knew I'd seen him lock her up and lecture her for three and four hours at a time, shouting at her, and coming out as red as fury. He knew I'd heard him say, 'I would give five hundred dollars if Lib were three inches taller.' He knew I'd seen him wandering at night, turning the pictures around backwards to the wall, and then wandering from bed to bed. Once he said, 'Pettie, let us go in and try Bessie's bed a little while.' And Mrs. Tilton was standing behind him with the pillows, crying. But now he said, 'My dear child'—and he took out his handkerchief and began to cry into it, 'Bessie,' he says, 'You are mistaken in the woman you place so much confidence in.' And then she, Mrs. Tilton, comes forward and says, 'Why shouldn't Bessie place confidence in me? She has no confidence in you—you have offered to ruin her.' And he turns his hot face to me and says, 'Bessie, my dear, did I ever attempt to take any improper liberties with you?' Said I, 'Yes, you did, but you called them *affinities.*' "

Uproarious laughter. Judge Neilson said, "Send

an officer round to see that order is kept." The sergeant said, "The officers are already stationed around the room, sir." Judge Neilson said, "I know they are, but they only stand there."

Mr. Evarts: "And then what, Miss Turner?"

"Well, Mr. Tilton says to me, 'Oh, my dear, you are excited—you are laboring under a false—mistake. The fact is this—Elizabeth is so in the habit of having men fondle her bosoms and her legs that she judges me by herself.' He pointed to a little red lounge in the parlor and he said he had seen Mrs. Tilton commit adultery with three friends of the family on that little red lounge. Mr. Tilton said to me, 'Now, Bessie, you know the truth—please go and sit down.' "

Mr. Evarts: "And did you?"

The audience could not be contained by a hundred policeman when she answered, "Yes, sir—but not on the little red lounge!"

There, I thought, we have not only put Theodore Tilton safely down into the abyss—we have covered him over. The danger is past. If Bessie had told such stories to Henry, of course he would have rushed to comfort poor Lib. Henry always goes extravagant for the wounded. Probably he did touch and caress a woman so bruised, so frightened, so set upon by that scalawag. Henry can't control himself when he is pushed into the proximity of hurt.

Harper's magazine was still with us: "Mr. Beecher's bearing has been that of a man who knew the dark shadow in which he moved was that of slander, not guilt." But other papers had had enough; one rag said that Mr. Beecher had not broken any commandments, especially "A new commandment I give unto you, that ye love one another"—no, said the editor, "he didn't break that one—he observed it, over and over again." In his study, preparing for his own assumption of the witness stand, Henry complained to Calvin and me, "The papers are slipping away from me—Bowles's Springfield *Republican*, Medill's *Tribune* in Chicago, and right here, Dana's *Evening Sun*—they are all dropping away from my side." I think it was Dana who had hurt him the most; Charles Dana wrote, "Henry Ward Beecher stands exposed as an adulterer and a fraud—his great genius and his Christian pretenses only make his sins the more horrible and revolting."

Old Rab tried to cheer up our failing patient with another newspaper, from Marseilles, France. Calvin had been through it with a red pencil, underlining and encircling: it said that three Anglican clergymen, "Vodull, Stilton, and Beecher," all had been seduced by "Madame Brecchestow, the mother of Uncle Tom."

Our constant occupation was fielding rumors. Tilton had shot Henry! The Woodhull was dead! Sunday supplements contained pirated letters and vicious cartoons. "The pistol shot of Booth caused a national sorrow no deeper and not so hopeless as the poisoned arrows of Victoria Woodhull." The congregation of Plymouth had voted Henry a salary of $100,000 that year, a sum without any parallel in the history of a religious body—but why, it was wondered, did an innocent man need such a lavish emergency fund? It was some comfort to us when we saw one reporter note that "Theodore Tilton values the female physique at the rate of $160 a lineal inch. He dreams of a woman like Woodhull." But the blacker Tilton got, the blacker Tilton got; it did not make Henry white.

I sat with him in the library, in the warm spring sun. He was fumbling with the buttons on his new white shirt, standing there in his old black pants, floppy as ever. He said, "You cannot hunt a stench. Odorous beasts are going up and down the streets, casting venom. Am I to run after every rat in creation?" I feared for him, feared for what he might do on the stand. As a boy he had been so poor in speaking—blushing, stammering, confused, so helpless and miserable, stuck in his catechism, confusing what was required with what was forbidden, the commandments jumbling up—once, according to legend, he stammered out, "Thou *shalt* commit adultery."

In the library he abandoned the buttons in despair. "This is *my* heresy trial." My heart sank to my shoes—and, at the same time, gladdened. The invocation of Father—it is apt, it is deeply right. Call on Father. His trial had stretched from the Great Valley all the way to New England; Father too had faced letters, printed communications, depositions, missives from members of his own congregation. The "Tilton" of that case was one Mr. Wilson, who cried, "Does Mr. Beecher presume to renovate Calvinism like a barn?" The official charge, booming down from forty years ago: "HERESY." Father had stood, in 1836, in the Darkness at Goshen, the mountains of Gilboa, the valley in 'Zekiel's vision, where the bones were many and dry. And Father had laughed in his sleeve, for he knew his Presbyterian management. All of his students at Lane had stood with him, as Plymouth now stood with Henry. Lyman Beecher vexed Mr. Wilson's soul and turned his pinching arguments into novel heresies; skipping about, nimble and strong, Father brought endless witnesses, a snowstorm of depositions, commentaries from Justin Martyr, Tatian, Irenaseus, Clement of Alexandria, Tertullian, Origen, Cyprian, Lactantius, Cyril of Jerusalem, Gregory, Ambrose, Augustine, Luther, Calvin, the Proceedings of the Synod of Dort, Tuckney, all the way to Dr. Witherspoon of South Carolina—with an ample side-dish of *usus loquendi.* Father laughed, "The fact is we outwinded them!"

Which I brought to Henry's recollection that morning—and all of which Henry dismissed with four words: "Father thought; I feel!" My heart took another dive for the ocean floor. Which Henry saw, and since he knew I was only trying to help him, to raise his spirits, he stopped with his hat in his hand. "I know, Tommy. I never left Father's side. I said to him, 'I know you're plagued good at twisting, but if you can twist your creed onto the Westminster Confession you can twist better than I think you can.' And you know what our father said to me, Tommy? He said, 'All my boys are smart, and one of them is impudent.'"

We embraced from afar. Eunice was waiting, it was time for court—where the spectators were double the usual number, milling around outside, for it had been trumpeted that today Henry Ward Beecher himself would face the world, under Oath.

The very taking of that Oath was the first surprise. Mr. Evarts, still in blue, said, "Mr. Beecher, will you be sworn?"

The officer presented the Bible in the usual manner, and Henry waved it away. He raised his right hand. The clerk said, "You solemnly swear that you—" and young Mr. Fullerton said, "One moment—I object to this, unless Mr. Beecher shall declare that he has conscientious scruples against swearing upon the Scripture." Henry said, "I do; I have conscientious scruples against swearing on the Bible." The clerk then said, "You solemnly affirm and declare—" but Mr. Evarts said, "No—he swears—he does not affirm and declare—he swears by the uplifted hand."

Henry said, "By the ever-living God."

And sat down to recount where he was born, where we had lived, the death of his mother, Roxana, in Litchfield, the family move to Boston, the fact that Father was a clergyman of the orthodox faith.

Q: "How numerous a family of children had your parents?"
A: "Thirteen born to them, eleven raised to man's estate."
Q: "How many of those were men and how many women?"
A: "Six boys and four girls."
Q: "Besides yourself? How do you make out eleven?"

Henry paused. "I have never been able to tell it right without counting, sir."

There was some laughter.

Q: "Now, Mr. Beecher, are your brothers all clergymen?"
A: "All of them."
Q: "And how many children do you and your wife have?"

Henry paused again, for some time; I wondered if he were trying to count his own children—given the circumstances, the paternity of the boy Ralph!, I was worried, until I saw what he was thinking, for with great solemnity he said, "Four with me and five waiting for me."

Henry's ordeal on the witness stand took several days, as we had all expected; the first few, of course, were under the direction of Mr. Evarts, from whom we had nothing to fear. But finally it became Mr. Evarts' obligation to say, "During the period of your acquaintance with Mrs. Tilton did any alienation of affection from her husband disclose itself to you?"

"The very contrary, the very contrary. It was a matter of some ridicule, her excessive addiction to her husband. It was the theme above all others that she seemed to love to talk about."

Q: "And you first took your book, *Norwood,* to her—to read it aloud and solicit her criticisms?"

A: "Yes, sir; I read portions of it."

Q: "Do you remember, in writing that book, of borrowing from the habit of the bird in hiding its nest a figure to illustrate the way that love might be concealed if it were necessary?"

A: "I do not, sir."

Q: "Let me refresh your memory with this passage"—here Mr. Evarts produced the novel, and read aloud from it:

It would seem as if, while her whole life centered upon his love, she would hide the precious secret by flinging over it vines and flowers, by mirth and raillery, as a bird hides its nest under tufts of grass, and behind leaves and vines as a fence against prying eyes.

"Mr. Beecher, do you recollect writing that?"

"I do not, sir. I have never read the book since the day it came out of the press. I presume it is my pen. It is in my book, with my name, and I presume it is mine." Henry looked down at Hatty in the audience, and said, "People used to accuse me of having written *Uncle Tom's Cabin*—until they read *Norwood.*"

Hatty smiled and the audience applauded.

Q: "Did you, among other things, present Mrs. Tilton with a picture called 'The Trailing Arbutus'?"

A: "I did."

Q: "And did you make her a present of that picture after reading to her from your book about 'the trailing arbutus' as 'the breath of love'?"

A: "I don't remember it, sir, but if it's there I guess I have got to stand it."

Q: "Don't you think that in some of the letters that counsel for the plaintiff has read that Mrs. Tilton was using words and phrases from your book?"

A: "I suppose she might have."

Q: "Such as 'My heart in its new sympathy for one abounds towards all. Does your heart bound towards all as it used to? So does mine. I am myself again.' What did you interpret that to mean?"

A: "I interpreted that to be the recovery from that state of despondency in which she had been."

Q: "'The bird has sung in my heart these four weeks. I did not dare tell you 'til I was sure.' How do you explain that one?"

A: "She did not dare tell me that she had gained a victory over herself, showing that she felt like a Christian woman, until she had put it to a proof—that she was seeking a spirit of love toward her husband, and of concord."

Q: "And during your entire acquaintance with Mrs. Tilton, had there ever been any undue personal familiarity between yourself and her?"

A: "Never."

Q: "Had you at any time, directly or indirectly, solicited improper favors from her as a woman?"

A: "Never."

Q: "Had you ever received improper favors from her?"

A: "It was a thing impossible to her—Never!"

When the Plymouth contingent burst into applause, Judge Neilson said, "Wait a moment, Mr. Evarts. This must not occur again. Sergeant, you will see to this, and if you find anyone disturbing the peace of the court, you will have your men remove him."

Mr. Evarts: "Now, Mr. Beecher, what happened when Mr. Moulton brought you to that fateful first interview of 30 December—the night he called you away from your prayer meeting?"

A: "My impression is that there was some allusion made to Mr. Tilton's difficulties with Mr. Bowen, but I cannot recall any details of the conversation. I reached the house. He then lived about five doors below St. Ann's, on Clinton Street, one of those brick houses. We entered, and he locked the front door, and said, 'Mr. Tilton is in the room above the parlor, waiting for you.' I said to him—supposing, wishing a witness, believing that we were going to have a business discussion—I said to him, 'I would rather you would go up with me, Mr. Moulton.' He said, 'You had better see Mr. Tilton alone.' So I went upstairs, knocked, and opened the door. Mr. Tilton was standing—"

At which point Henry did a rather remarkable thing—he changed the tense of his verbs:

"—Mr. Tilton is standing. Two windows front out onto Clinton Street. A bureau is between them, and the gaslight there. Tilton upon the far side of the bureau. He meets me in the most stately manner, points to a chair, asks me to sit down. I do so. He draws out from his pocket a little piece of paper"— Henry rummaged in his vest pocket, among some other

150

papers, and pulled out a small envelope—"just about this size, a little narrower. He says, 'I have summoned you to this interview on matters of importance. I revoke and recall the letter I sent to you by Mr. Bowen.'"

Mr. Evarts, catching the drama in it, shifted his tenses as well: "How do you respond?"

"With a bow. He then begins to allude to Mr. Bowen, and Mr. Bowen's treatment of him—not going into it in any considerable detail, but characterizing it as very base and very treacherous. Then he charges me with having an understanding with Mr. Bowen in these matters, and furthering them—that I have accepted injurious stories of him, that I have reported them again, that I have advised against him. At this point I am disposed to make some explanation—but he warns me to be silent. I am. Then Theodore proceeds to say I have not only injured him in his business relations, his reputation, and his prospects, but that I have also insinuated myself into his family, during his absence. I have wrought him mischief there. In a sense superseded him and taken his place. His wife looks to me rather than to him. I have caused her to transfer her affections from him to me—in an inordinate measure. Now his family is well-nigh destroyed. I have suffered my own wife, and also his mother-in-law, to conspire for the separation of the family. I have corrupted Elizabeth, teaching her to lie and deceive him."

Henry stopped, as if the drama were too much for him. Then he went on in a low voice: "I had married them—I, all the long years before, in 1855, I had married them." He pondered, as if waiting for a cue from Mr. Evarts, but then he found it in himself: "I had tied the knot in the sanctuary of God, by which they were bound together in an inseparable love, and now—now I had reached out my hand to untie that knot, to loose them one from the other. And then—then he goes on to say that not only have I done this, but that I have made overtures to her, of an improper character. He draws the paper"—and here Henry presented his envelope, holding it there in front of his large chest—"and he reads to me what purports to be the statement of his wife to him. And he says he will tear it up. That there should never be a line or letter against the reputation of his wife. And with that he takes the letter"—Henry takes the envelope, tears it once, tears it twice, tears it three times and lets the pieces float in the air and flutter to the floor.

"'Theodore,' I say, 'this is a dream. Elizabeth could never have made in writing a statement so untrue.' Says he, 'Go see her for yourself.' I turn and go out of the door and walk downstairs, meeting Mr. Moulton at the foot of the stairs. He says to me, 'Are you going down to see Mrs. Tilton?' 'Why,' say I, 'how do you know, for I am just on my way?' He takes his hat—I think he had his overcoat on—and he goes to the door to let me out, and it is locked, and he feels in his pocket for the key—and it's not there, so he turns and goes back to the clothes-stand in the hall, and takes the key from the drawer, saying, sort of *sotto voce*, that they did not want an interruption during this interview, and he unlocks the door, and we go out on our way."

Q: "Do you in any manner invite Mr. Moulton to go with you to Mrs. Tilton's?"

A: "No, sir; I don't want him."

Q: "Do you in any manner inform him of your destination before he asks you whether you are going to Mrs. Tilton's?"

A: "I don't."

Q: "And he attends you to her door?"

A: "He does."

Q: "And on the way do you converse, does anything pass between you?"

A: "I cannot recall it, sir. I remember speaking something of the storm that was just breaking in the sky—a winter snow-storm."

Q: "And when you reach the door, does he go in with you?"

A: "Yes he does, but stays downstairs, as previous. The housekeeper—I suppose by her dress and appearance, to be the housekeeper—"

Q: "But is she a lady whom you personally know?"

A: "I think not. She tells me to go upstairs to Mrs. Tilton's room. I do. I knock on the door. It is open. I go in from the door of the hall and come, therefore, almost immediately to the bed, for the folding-doors are open."

Q: "Is there any other person, any person other than yourself and Mrs. Tilton in either of the rooms, to your knowledge, during the time of your interview with her?"

A: "No, sir."

Q: "Describe the scene as you enter the room."

Henry ponders a moment. "The bed dressed in pure white. Mrs. Tilton dressed in pure white. Her face as white as the bed, lying a little above level, reclined on pillows, her hands in this form on her breast"—Henry put his hands up, palm to palm—"I draw a chair, and sit down. Her eyes are closed."

Q: "Is she asleep?"
A: "She is as one dead, and yet she is living. I—"

Tilton's attorney, young Fullerton, rises. "We object, Your Honor, to the conversation between this witness and Mrs. Tilton."

Judge Neilson says, "I think you will have to take it. We have in evidence that the witness obtained from Mrs. Tilton that evening a letter. The fact has been proved pretty clearly. I think we shall have to take it, as a part of the act of receiving the letter."

Mr. Evarts: "Proceed, Mr. Beecher."

Mr. Fullerton objects again, saying the conversation was no part of the *res gestae*. The testimony imputes authorization for the visit by Mr. Tilton. Mr. Beecher was not an authorized party from Mr. Tilton—"yet," Mr. Fullerton sighs, "I see that Your Honor will allow it, is disposed to admit this evidence, so we must record our objection and exception."

Mr. Evarts, again: "Proceed, Mr. Beecher."

Henry is all in his element; he has father's heresy trial somewhere far, far behind him now, for he is in Lib Tilton's bedroom: "I say to her, in a whisper, 'Elizabeth, I have just seen your husband. I thought it was to be a business discussion, but he has charged me with alienating your affections from him. He has charged me that I have corrupted your simplicity. He has also charged me—with—attempting improprieties—'" and Henry's eyes spill over, the scene is too much for him, and he apologizes: "I—it is a hard thing—I cannot express myself very clearly—I ask, 'Are these things so, Elizabeth? Are they so?'"

Henry takes out his handkerchief and wipes his eyes. "She—she—there is the faintest quiver, and tears trickle down her cheek, but no answer. I say to her, 'Theodore says that you—you, Elizabeth—have charged me with making improper advances. Have you stated all these things?'" Again, Henry reaches to the floor beside the chair, as if he were on his throne in Plymouth Church; he brings up a nosegay of violets. Refreshed somewhat, he puts the flowers carefully down, next to one of the torn scraps of envelope. "She opens her eyes. She says, 'My friend, I could not help it.' And there she lies, all white. I say, 'Could not help it, Elizabeth? Why? You know that these things are not true.' She replies, 'Oh, Mr. Beecher, I was wearied out. I have been—I have been wearied with his importunities. He made me think that if I would confess love to you it would help him to confess to me his alien affections.' And I, 'But Elizabeth, this is a charge of attempting improper things. You know that that is not true.' 'Yes,' she says, 'it is not true, but what can I do?' 'Do? You can take it back again.' She hesitates, and I do not understand her hesitation. She says she is so afraid of her husband. She says she is willing to do it if it will not harm her husband and make him angry with her. I say, 'Do you have paper?' She points to the secretary in the other room, which stands between the windows. I go there, and take some note paper, pen, and ink. I bring them to the bed. She raises herself and begins to write—'Wearied with importunities and weakened by sickness—' Oh, the poor, dear child!" And Henry is again in tears.

Mr. Evarts waits a decent interval. "During the writing, Mr. Beecher, do you in any manner dictate or suggest any of the language used?"

"No, sir. She reads it over, to herself, looks it over, and then holds out her pen for some more ink, which I have in my hand, and she adds a postscript, and signs with her full name. I do not suggest or request anything additional. It is of her own mind."

"Do you say anything to her as to any injury that might come to *you* from this charge?"

"I do, sir. Some rumor of this matter might come to mischief-makers, might get into the church. But the main thing on my mind—I tell her that no woman can make such a charge without injuring herself and doing injury to her children."

"How long is this interview, Mr. Beecher?"

"It seemed to me about ten hours—it was probably only one half-hour. I suddenly see her weakened condition, close to break-down—oh, it is a pitiable thing—and it bespeaks a great sorrow in the household. And I suddenly see, too, that Theodore at least sees me as the occasion of it, although I have never suspected it. And so I withdraw, and go back to Mr. Moulton's house. At the time I feel Mr. Moulton is a friend to both sides, and when I have just come from these two scorching interviews, I for the first time give air, at Mr. Moulton's house, to the pent-up feelings that I had. I am one upon whom trouble works inwardly, making me outwardly silent, but reverberating in the chambers of my soul. When at length I do speak it is a pent-up flood and pours without measure or moderation. I inherit a tendency to sadness—the remains in me of a—a positive hypochondria in my father—"

So, I think, Tom is wrong: Father is not far off

from Henry. Indeed, Henry looks out the courtroom windows, looks out, as if reaching for Father.

"What do you do and say at Mr. Moulton's house?"

"Oh, sir, I walk about the room in great agitation and great self-condemnation. I say to Mr. Moulton that I cannot conceive of anything for which a man should blame himself more utterly than to intrude upon a household and to be the means of breaking it up. My idea of friendship and love is that it gives strength—and I had always supposed that my presence in the Tilton family was giving strength to them all, that it was a blessing to the children, that it was a help to Mrs. Tilton, and that it was not without a beneficial influence to Theodore. This comes upon me like a thunder-clap. I am amazed by it. I am bewildered by it."

We are all watching, watching for a sign, a lie, somewhere a falseness, but there is no sign. Henry Ward Beecher is telling the truth—his face intent on the calm regard of Mr. Evarts. The courtroom seems to be, itself, lost in Henry's amazement, lost in his bewilderment, for it still is bewilderment. Henry does an odd thing. He puts his leg over the arm of the witness chair. "Mr. Moulton sitting like this, just this way," and Henry Ward Beecher's Puritan shoe, its big buckle swinging over the violets on the floor, he does not look at all like Von Moltke, "Our Mutual Friend." But suddenly he sounds like him: " 'Why, there is no doubt about it, Mr. Beecher—Elizabeth Tilton loves your little finger more than she does Mr. Tilton's whole body!' "

Henry brings his leg away and puts his foot down beside its partner. "I accept it. I have no means of contradiction. I say to myself, 'It has been a smoldering fire, burning, concealed, and I knew nothing about it.' I feel too ashamed to say, 'It is not my fault.' I feel the impulse. I suppose every gentleman will understand that I feel it, the impulse to say, 'I ought to have foreseen—I was the oldest man, the oldest person—I was the one who had the experience, I—she was but a child. If she did not know that the tendrils of her affection were creeping up upon me, I ought to have known it.' I believe I expressed myself without measure on that subject. I had always thought of her as a saint-like person, and the conflict that now was in my mind in respect to her as one who had been broken down, and had brought false charges against me, and now taken them back, and now was near death it seemed, and acting in a manner almost like one who was bereft of reason, and the two images—they plunge downward—I cannot understand it. Oh, the consciousness of being loved always produces a reaction in my nature—a sense of unworthiness, sadness, and even a sense—of—sinfulness." Henry sits there, lost in himself. He sits for the better part of a minute, in silence. Then: "It is—it seems harder to me—so much harder, because the implication is that I have made use of my reputation, and my position as the head of a great Church, and my relation to the community—that all those, aside from my mere personal action, have gone to overshadow and injure Theodore. That he has occasion to think that I had done him wrong in the matter of Mr. Bowen, that I had counselled Mr. Bowen to cashier him, especially after the more violent articles, inspired by Victoria Woodhull—I am ashamed to be obliged to admit it. But that I had done my Theodore any intentional wrong in his family—in his own family—that I deny.

But, unintentionally, I have wronged him there, it is very evident, it seems to me, from the condition of Mrs. Tilton. And so Moulton and I go over this same ground, a good many times—and Mr. Moulton is far less severe with me than I am with myself, and at times he deprecates my own strong language against myself, and says that if I could only—that if Theodore could only hear what he has heard, he is satisfied that it would remove from his mind animosity and the conviction that I am seeking his ruin. 'Well,' says I, I say to Frank, 'State what you see and hear—I have opened my heart to you.' Says he, 'Write—write these statements, or some of them, to Mr. Tilton.' And at first I think I will, but I am in a whirl. 'Well,' says he, 'let me write it,' and he sits down, at the table, but our conversation does not stop. I amplify and go on, and finally he says to me, 'Well, I will tell Mr. Tilton so and so, as a sort of interpretation of what I have been saying, and I say, 'All right,' and he makes a memorandum of it. And then I go on from point to point, and sometimes he says, 'What about so and so?' and I go on talking, profusely and long, and he jots down another memorandum about it. When he gets through, Moulton rises up from the table and gathers the papers, and as a sort of an afterthought he comes to me and says, 'Sign this,' and I say, 'No, I cannot sign a letter I have not written.' So, far away from the text of the last sheet, I write down, 'I have entrusted this in confidence to Moulton,' and sign that sentence. And go out."

It is grave; it is a tremendous session. Henry Ward Beecher leaves the stand to tumultuous applause; the crowd is entirely his. A crush of well-wishers impends towards and around him.

The battle, I think, is won. For months now he has shown no sign, no sign of weakness, and now even his weakness is his strength. I am in a mist of aching, ancient victory.

But Mr. Fullerton has been scrutinizing Henry closely—young Mr. Fullerton, who waves away Theodore Tilton with a notebook, Mr. Fullerton slowly smiling, sitting there in his mulberry seersucker and navy vest, Mr. Fullerton, absently pulling at his ear.

On the third day he began his cross-examination. We were having a sudden burst of summer, an oppressive heat filling Brooklyn Court—a heat that seemed to intensify when a dozen men broke in and flowed through the room to take seats reserved for the reporters. A lively scuffle. It was the largest crowd yet, including a Minister to Mexico, some Judges, and the Envoy Extraordinary of Japan, Mr. Kiyonari.

Fullerton approached Henry warily. "Why did you keep silent for so long about this matter, Mr. Beecher?"

"A man has a right to concealment. The soul has no more business to go stark naked down the street than a man has to go stark naked in regards to his body. The man that has no great silence in him, no reserve, is not half a man—he leaks at the mouth."

Fullerton said, "The plaintiff has testified that in these interviews you were so awe-struck by the truth of his accusation—not that you had made improper advances, sir, but that you were guilty of the criminal debauchery of his wife—that you said you would commit suicide. You said that you had some powder on your library table, a medicine that results in death. Mr. Tilton said you told him you would take a powder."

"Take a powder?" said Henry. "I once heard a man from Nevada tell me he would take a powder, meaning he was leaving town. My, is that not extraordinary—to take a powder—"

"Mr. Beecher, please."

"Oh, I want to get at just what you want, Mr. Fullerton, and if I seem sometimes to evade you it is because I am either dull or am anxious to tell the truth."

"Had you any powder on your library table?"

"Sir, the only powder that I know of was gunpowder upstairs."

"Mr. Beecher, were you contemplating taking your life?"

"Oh, no, sir, not that I would take my life—that God would. So many Sundays, I have thought, 'This is my last.' I know you refer to my letter to Mrs. Tilton, when I said I did not expect to be alive many days. Well, sir, that statement stands connected with a series of symptoms that I first experienced in 1856. The Frémont Campaign. I would speak in the open air three hours at a time, three days in the week. And I felt I might give way, have apoplexy or—my greatest fear, sir, always—paralysis."

Mr. Fullerton was watching him.

"On two or three occasions while preaching I was sure I would fall. It is why, at Plymouth Church, I removed the pulpit and installed a chair, for often I must sit, to regather my strength."

The chair?, the throne, I had always thought—I stared at Hatty, sitting with Catharine, my great sisters, united in principle and devotion to their brother—my half-sisters, my half-brother—Roxana's grave blossomed . . . love never dies. . . .

"Very often, sir, I came near falling in the streets. A hundred times I have approached a podium thinking death was very near my hand. The doctors have said to me, 'You must stop work.' So I stopped going to doctors. But I read the best books. They make three points: good sleep, good digestion, work. How do I get, I have asked myself, the most work out of my body without permanently impairing it? In '63, in England, I knew I was on the edge of stroke. I have this awful fear of paralysis. I have felt it these last years with special force. I know that Theodore has said of me, 'He is courageous before a multitude—a coward before an individual.' Not so, sir. I am no coward. But I am fearful before God. I have lived a public life. Public men are bees working in a glass hive, and curious spectators enjoy themselves in watching every secret movement as if it were a study in natural history. But, after these four years, my soul is a terrible house of imagery. I go down into the dungeon of my own experience, and come up not without shudder and chill from those dark chambers and hidden cavities and slimy recesses. And, suddenly, to be stricken paralytic—to be mute, helpless, incarcerate in one's own living body, alive in a house of death—"

"Mr. Beecher—"

"I apologize. I am not in a logical mood. I did not measure my words. I am afraid I may even have mixed my metaphors. But I shall gradually learn to behave, sir."

"If we can pause on just one metaphor—'nest-hiding'—"

"Mr. Fullerton, I simply thought 'nest-hiding' meant that Mrs. Tilton was hiding the troubles of her own household. Sir, I hold the most sacred of human institutions to be the family. All my life I have preached *Family* as the incarnation of the divine spirit."

"But you hold the head of one family, Mr. Tilton, to be a base calumnator?"

"No, Mr. Fullerton, no. I loved him like a son. He seemed to me to be a splendid specimen of a man, in many respects, and he had qualities so utterly different from mine, and in which I thought that he surpassed. By the principle of counterparts, I suppose, I took to him very strongly. He did seem to me to have given a new meaning to friendship— and I think he still does."

There was a bubble of laughter from the audience, and I peered through it at Henry: he was suddenly a little boy, full of wonder, and simultaneously a wise old codger who has been holding back the "clincher." I thought to myself, the man does not know who he is!—and then I thought, the man knows exactly who he is!—and what's more, he knows exactly who we are.

Mr. Fullerton reversed engines. "You have spoken here of impending death, but you wrote in *Norwood*:

The most solemn hour of human experience is not that of death, but of Life—for the first time, when one so loves that love is sacrifice, death of self, resurrection and glory—then man is brought into harmony with the whole universe, and like him who beheld the seventh heaven, hears things unlawful to be uttered."

Henry said, "I wrote that?"
"It is here in your book."
"Well, it is a delightful idea. I am glad to own to it."
"Mr. Beecher, you have published perhaps too many books to remember—"
"Oh, yes, I had two volumes of sermons published, unauthorized, in England. I had sired two children and wasn't aware of it!"
Watch out, Henry, I thought—my own mind spinning again with the paternity of Ralph—watch out—
Henry was immediately cognizant. "Sir, you see what my language does to me. I do *slop over* sometimes. Had I been the evil man Mr. Tilton now represents, I should have been calmer and more prudent in allowing Mr. Moulton to take down my thoughts. But my horror of the evil imputed to me filled me with morbid intensity at the very shadow of it."
Mr. Fullerton, hiking up his mulberry trousers from his shiny black boots, said, "You have written:

Acquaintance is May; friendship—that is June; then brother and sisterhood, July; and then August, love; but July and August are so much alike that no one can tell where one stops and the other begins.

Tell me, Mr. Beecher: Was your relationship with Mrs. Tilton July or August?"

Henry looked at his Puritan shoes. "I suspect, Mr. Fullerton, you will not be satisfied until I call it January and May."

Fullerton, startled, glanced at the stenographer to make sure it was recorded. Then he said, "Did you not proclaim that it is the obligation of clergy to be men before ministers—that they should"—and he leaned on the words—"that one should 'thrust and lunge and pour his manhood into the congregation'?"

"Oh, but Mr. Fullerton, I only said it at Yale."

The audience immensely enjoyed it. Meanwhile Mr. Fullerton was building another trap: "You wrote, 'I never know how to worship until I know how to love; trust the heart's instincts, whose channels you may appoint but whose flowing is beyond your control.' Was your 'flowing' beyond your control with Elizabeth Tilton, sir?"

"Oh, Mr. Fullerton—"

"Mr. Beecher, you wrote, 'I think God will not blame me for my acts with her. I know that at present it would be utterly impossible for me to justify myself before man.' Yet here, in the court of the City of Brooklyn—are you not trying to justify yourself before man? You who have made 'paroxysmal kiss' a phrase bandied about in the street. Justify yourself before women, sir. You have written: 'Women, who have such need of love, ought not to find it hard to come to Jesus Christ, and put their arms about His neck, and tell Him, with gushing love, that they give themselves, body and soul, into

His keeping.' *Body* and soul, Mr. Beecher?"

"In Christ's keeping."

"This scandal—did not an intimate of yours say it would knock the *Life of Christ* higher than a kite?"

"I have enough trouble accounting for my own words, sir."

"Mr. Beecher, I wish to read to you a passage from a great book, to see whether or not you agree with it. Listen, sir:

> The seducer! Playing upon the most tender passions, he betrays innocence. How? By its tenderest faculties, by its trust, by its unsuspecting faith. Far down, the very bottom of infamy, the ghastliness of death, the last spasm of horrible departure, the awful thunder of final doom. When one knows such things as these are in eternal wait for the seducer, one thanks God there is a judgment and there is a Hell.

Do you agree with it, sir?"

Henry looked at him blankly. "Did I write that one, too?"

"Yes, Mr. Beecher, those words are yours—written thirty years ago, in Indianapolis. How can we trust what you remember saying when you cannot remember what you write?"

Henry moaned. "Lo, those thirty years ago."

"Do you disown your words?"

"Mr. Fullerton, I am made of sterner stuff."

"Or more pliable material." Mr. Fullerton was alive with the chase: "Did you say that the sexual expression of love was just as natural as the spiritual?"

"Did I say that?"

"Did you?"

"It sounds like The Woodhull to me."

Applause.

"Did Moulton say, 'You have committed a criminal connection with Mrs. Tilton,' and then when you went to get her retraction, Mr. Moulton escorted you there? I don't see how such two acts were performed. How could Mr. Moulton do such two contradictory things?"

"Mr. Moulton is not a fool, sir; he is a very sagacious man—"

"Oh, he is?"

"I merely mean that as a form of negative. It is intolerable to be asked these questions. Before Almighty God, sir—words do kill. Regard your tone, Mr. Fullerton. I do wonder, sir, that you approach me with such a—tone."

I glanced at Mr. Evarts, sitting cool, and I understood why he had so often been compared to Henry Clay. Mr. Evarts had not once risen to object; he knew his human nature as well as his law.

Henry said, "Mr. Fullerton, I am so constantly afraid of doing wrong that I sometimes do wrong"—a massive tremor came up from his Puritan shoes, running up through his black trousers, running across his breast and shoulders—his body wept without anger: "I sometimes do wrong just from my anxiety to do right!"

Mr. Fullerton stood there, with his legal papers. To no one in particular he said, "It is an unfortunate condition to get into." He said the words like an echo. Suddenly, for the first time, Mr. Fullerton has to contend with Henry Ward Beecher's innocence.

Henry stared at him, his jowls loose but his jaw set.

Mr. Fullerton said, "I did not mean to rebuke you."

Henry leaned down for his flowers. "When you shall find a heart to rebuke the twining morning-glory, you may rebuke me."

That was perhaps too much. It gave Mr. Fullerton one last fire: "You mean to tell us, Mr. Beecher, you were willing to put that retraction of Mrs. Tilton in your pocket, and leave the husband in ignorance of the fact that you had been vindicated against the charge?"

Henry's whole soul leaned out of his twining morning-glory, his trailing arbutus, his roses and violets and moral hollyhocks—his face alive with floral splendour: "Not at all, sir; I was perfectly willing to put the retraction in my pocket, and leave the husband to find out the retraction where he had found out the charge!"

Again, applause in the courtroom.

Judge Neilson gavelled.

Mr. Fullerton, perspiring in his mulberry seersucker: "But you were anxious, of course, to secure and enjoy his good opinion, were you not?"

"The same anxiety that I have towards you, Mr. Fullerton."

"Towards me, Mr. Beecher?"

"Indeed. I much prefer your good opinion to your bad."

"But, sir, I am counsel for the plaintiff."

"This trial will end—someday."

"But, Mr. Beecher, the issue here is timeless, it has no season, it is as clear as the Holy Scriptures—"

"I do not deny it, Mr. Fullerton, I affirm it."

"But Mr. Beecher, should this proceeding discover that you are guilty—"

"Oh, I discovered that long ago, sir. We are all guilty. All of us who live in the world, we are guilty of one thing or another."

"But the guilt alleged here, Mr. Beecher—it is the—it partakes of the Original Sin—" Mr. Fullerton turned back to Henry and said, "Adam and Eve were guilty, Mr. Beecher, were they not?"

"Oh, I fear they were, Mr. Fullerton."

"And what were Adam and Eve guilty of, Mr. Beecher?"

"Adam and Eve were guilty of—inexperience."

They looked, long, at each other.

Finally Henry said, "May I make a statement, Mr. Fullerton? Please allow me to speak for a few moments, without interruption."

Now Fullerton didn't know which way to turn—he was looking, looking for a crack, somewhere a fatal flaw, he had to find it. Adam and Eve, guilty of *inexperience?* So Mr. Fullerton decided, right there, to give Henry Ward Beecher enough rope. "Speak away, Mr. Beecher—speak away!"

"I only mean to say that these four years I have not been hunted as the eagle is hunted, I have not been hunted as a lion is hunted, I have not been pursued even as wolves and foxes. I have been pursued as if I were a maggot in a rotten corpse. I have about come to the state of mind that I don't care for you or anybody else. Well, you know that is not so. I do care. And I don't. I am tired of you, Mr. Fullerton. I am tired of the world. I am tired of men who make newspapers and men who read them. People look upon this trial here as if it were a game of battledore and shuttlecock, as if being tried were nothing but being tossed in the air by two clever fellows, and as if I ought to like it. Is it possible for a man to live as long as I have, and as openly, and to have acted upon so large a theatre, and been agitated by such events that shake the world—and be so utterly misconceived? Oh, tomorrow morning, it will be said in the journals, 'Well, Mr. Beecher—how rhetorically he managed the matter.' I am questioned and questioned and questioned. And all my friends here—all these wonderful friends who have supported me, and testified for me, and given me their cash—all that friendship—it seems to me now—it seems to me the humane effort of good men to drag an *ass* out of the pit."

The stillness in the courtroom was close, very close, all around us. Henry shook his head. "Mr. Fullerton, I never meant to injure Theodore in his family. But I did do wrong to him in his business relations, and I sought to undermine his influence on the newspaper because of his articles on Free Love—but I thought then, as I think now—Love is not Free—oh, no, sir, no"—each word came out like a cannonball boomed over a lake at dusk—"Love is not free."

In the courtroom many of the women, and some of their husbands, were in tears.

Henry's massive frame was so unbearably still, as if he were carved there. Mr. Fullerton himself seemed almost to want to go to him, but he stood quietly away with that expression on his young face, a silent cry of 'Exception!—Exception!—this must not be—Never!—not, not the *law*!'

Henry moaned, "It is terrible to be loved!" Like an epitaph.

Next to me Harriet Beecher Stowe had buried her face in Calvin's hand; poor Old Rab was turning his upper body away, away from his hand in his wife's lips and teeth. Two rows forward, the wife of Henry Ward Beecher, Love is not free, Eunice Bullard Beecher, it is terrible to be loved, Eunice all in black—her tight smile, like arithmetic.

1875, God discovers Brooklyn.

On the third of May, Lib Tilton suddenly stood up. She had been in court for several sessions, and now she was standing in the front, with clear eyes, reading a statement: "Judge Neilson, I ask the privilege from you for a few words in my own behalf. My soul cries out before you, and the gentlemen of the jury, that they beware how, if they bring in a divided verdict, they will consign to my children a false and irrevocable stain upon their mother. I declare solemnly before you, without fear of men and by faith in God, that I am innocent of the crimes charged against me. I would like to tell my whole sad story truthfully—to acknowledge the frequent falsehoods wrung from me by compulsion."

All the lawyers, at both tables, were on their feet. The unveiled lady! The Judge declared a recess, and Elizabeth Tilton was surrounded by the press: "Theodore's hatred for Mr. Beecher has existed these many years, and the determination to ruin Mr. Beecher has been the one aim of his life." Lib's voice failed her and a lady friend had to read aloud: "Never have I been guilty of adultery with Henry Ward Beecher, in thought or deed; nor has he ever offered to me an indecorous or improper proposal."

The delay, the astonishment, the procedural ramblings—another day was wiped out. But it will be Mr. Evarts, I thought, Mr. Evarts who will save Henry. And he did, immaculate in a white suit:

"Everybody has been trying Everybody. Europe has been trying America. Manhattan has been trying Brooklyn. The infidels have been trying the Christians." He proceeded to plead for decency, public decency: Mr. Tilton's blow would not be struck at Mr. Beecher but at our own wives and daughters. Mr. Evarts spent a full day on "The Letter of Contrition," in which Moulton had put down the scalpel and picked up the pen. Mr. Evarts pointed out the hasty expressions spread over a long conversation, eagerly grasped at by someone anxious to record the worst language he could possibly select from the excited utterances of a man under the influence of deepest feeling. This was no deliberate dictation—"I can't ask nothing"—with the "t" on "can't" crossed out. The entire card had changed when Tilton published it with all the punctuation regularized. Besides, it was a trick from the start— which is why Mr. Beecher did not sign it, why he "entrusted" it to Moulton. "And why," Mr. Evarts boomed, "why did Theodore Tilton destroy the one thing that would have settled the case? Where is the logic of taking out the original letter of confession—why destroy that and preserve all the others? The most important paper in the case is missing; everything else, no matter how tangential, is preserved."

Mr. Evarts exercised a power over the audience that was perfect craftsmanship. He had an Old World elegance and a New World intensity; he seemed to be something made, mined in Louisville and hammered in Florence. I thought to myself: what a wonderful thing to be able to buy Mr. Evarts. Like a color-opiate or a Persian rug. To purchase his brain, manner, and power. Henry is bankrolled into Heaven; war is not a soldier-boy, it is *materiel*.

"Witnesses are to be weighed, not counted." Tilton met fatal obstacles, enumerated before us like valuable coins. The unblemished character and unspotted purity of the lady! The four successive years, after the pretended knowledge of the crime, that Tilton had falsified, both orally and in writing, falsified the very accusation that this court was supposed to endorse; the obstacle, opposed to all human observation and experience, was that Theodore cohabited with the alleged adulteress as a pure and unsullied wife for all those months, those years, after she had polluted the marriage bed. "You know that charge is false. Blood does not lie!" Facts at war with accusations; history obliterating charges. Dishonor after the fact! To expose in nakedness the confidence of conjugal affection—to bray it from the very housetops! "Well now, justice stands, though the woman fall. Down with justice. Down with woman. Up with letters! Which is best to publish? *There's* a good one. But it don't read well. *That*—oh, put *that* in. This one's fine. But maybe it don't read right. Fix it; strike that sentence out. Make it *read!*

Garbled letters, infamous purpose, culled with a view to falsehood. Send them to the world. Send them to the Springfield *Republican*."

Mr. Evarts was sad. "I have never been able to comprehend precisely why it was thought needful to publish these letters—other than Theodore Tilton's infatuation with himself. Mrs. Tilton writes to him:

Now, tonight, I give myself to you—my best, my worst, just as I am. Take me once again into your confidence; bear with me my follies as I do yours. I consecrate myself to you so long as I shall live. Forgive all my infirmities. Help me to overcome, to find victory. Wilt thou? So will I of you, if you permit. Then the fountain is unsealed and we flow together!

"This from the bed of debauchery, the bed of lust, a woman who fears her husband is losing the foundations of his faith, and humbly, modestly, appeals to him:

Oh, my Theodore, may I not persuade you to love the Lord Jesus Christ? Do not let this entreaty estrange us more, for my pillow oft is wet with tears and prayers. Do have patience with me, for as the time remains to us, I feel as though my heart will break if I do not speak to you—not that I am right in any sense, and you are wrong—God forbid!—but we are one in feeling, especially while God blesses us with our dear children. I once again ask forgiveness if I have offended you by showing my heart. Our dear baby grows finely—

"Just imagine a woman, right out of the hotbed of adultery, writing this! Literature has got to stop somewhere!

"We have on our hands a Transcendental Adultery. Now, 'Transcendental' is a long word; it begins nowhere and ends everywhere. Twenty-five years ago the word came into great vogue under the lead of a great thinker, now famous, Mr. Ralph Waldo Emerson. It got into the language of young women and some students. But what does 'Transcendental' mean? Well, on one of the Mississippi River steamboats, when a parcel of eminent divines was returning from a general convention of the Presbyterian Church, they were in a high discussion about orthodoxy, and the old faith, and Transcendentalism. A gentleman who enjoyed their conversation still felt puzzled. So he ventured to ask the divine in whom he had the greatest confidence, 'Now, what does Transcendentalism mean?' 'Well,' says the divine, 'that is a question more easily asked than answered.' They were passing by a bluff on the river. Says the Doctor, 'Do you see that bluff there? Do you see how pierced it is with swallows' holes?' 'Yes, I see that.' 'Well now,' says the Doctor of Divinity, 'you take away all that bluff and leave nothing but swallows' holes, and you have Transcendentalism.'

"That is this adultery. Take away pollution of soul, prostitution of intellect, defilement of body—and there you have it: Theodore Tilton's Transcendental Swallows' Holes."

After the laughter of the audience, Mr. Evarts drew himself up into elegant conscience: "Save Brooklyn! Save Beecher—

An eagle towering in his pride of place
Hawked at and killed by mousing owls!

Say to America—This far shalt thou come, but no farther—the midnight plottings of cruel craft must cease forever! Oh, what a spectacle has been presented in the city of churches! Day by day Henry Ward Beecher has passed along our streets with his brave and true wife, to meet the unmerited indignity. Strong men have been touched with mingled pity and wrath at the sight, and women have turned to weep. Posterity will avenge this outrage. What you do here shall never die. Do you—and this is what the trial here in Brooklyn finally presents to you—Do you believe in Henry Ward Beecher? Do you believe in your own families? Do you believe in God?"

But, oh gentlemen, said Mr. Fullerton, in his finest hour, Mr. Fullerton chastened away from his mulberry seersucker into a prurient green: "Christianity has stood a great many worse catastrophes than the loss of Henry Ward Beecher. There is no fear for progress of Christian influence; the Church will survive. Mr. Dimmesdale, in *The Scarlet Letter,* asks, 'Hester, hast thou found peace?' In response, she 'smiled dreamily, looking down upon her bosom, which contained the scarlet letter 'A' signifying Adulteress.' And the defendant's very own brother, Mr. Thomas Kinnicut Beecher—"

I froze—I froze in the summer day of the courtroom—what?—what?—

"The Rev. T. K. Beecher, of Elmira, has written that 'there is no proof as yet of any offense on Henry's part. Moulton & Co. are witnesses. Even Mrs. Stanton can only declare hearsay. We shall not probably ever get the facts, and I'm glad of it. If Mr. and Mrs. Tilton are brought into court, nothing will be revealed. Perjury for good reasons is, with advanced thinkers, no sin.' "

Stirring in my sweat, ready to rise: this cannot be, this cannot be—I wrote that, months ago, to

Isabella, and how on earth did she get it relayed to this courtroom? Well, no, that's an easy question. But I have already registered my protest twenty years ago, and when I wrote my sister, "Perjury for good reasons is, with advanced thinkers, no sin"— when I wrote that, I was thinking of Theodore telling Bessie Turner that sexual intimacy was, with advanced thinkers, no sin—those words were my irony, not my opinion—

Rise to say that? Like Lib Tilton without her veil?

It was no matter, it got lost. My letter did not even occasion a glance from Eunice, quite used to Beecherish distractions—though when I went over the transcripts later I discovered that Mr. Fullerton had also played fast and loose with Nathaniel Hawthorne—Hawthorne said Hester looked down "drearily," not "dreamily," and he never wrote that the scarlet letter "A" signified Adulteress—young Mr. Fullerton, not Old Mr. Hawthorne, was the author of that—

Isabella, words do kill! But one of the jurors was rising. He said, "We have been forced to follow carefully these long and tedious proceedings, obliged to neglect our vocations, to disregard the ties of family and of home, with no other compensation than the pittance we are receiving. All these things are sufficiently grievous to us without being obliged to listen to innuendos that we will be swayed from an honest consideration of the case."

Purloined letters (especially "A"), breaches of confidence, and—and now Jury Tampering.

Judge Neilson gave them their charge. The burden of proof rests upon the plaintiff. "The evidence," says Judge Neilson, "should be such as to carry conviction to the mind of a prudent and discreet man." He drones on in the awful heat of the afternoon. "We are wont to say that all suitors are treated alike—"

Suitors?

"—and in most respects they are. But in a case of this character a man grown old in prayer and pious service has *prima facie* the benefit of a presumption that the mere man of the world has not." Judge Neilson started to say more, then stopped himself—or the applause stopped him.

Applause? Thunder! The failures and inspiration of family are washed away in it.

Henry has rescued the name of Beecher—America needs it.

The saloons were jammed. The jury did not report immediately—it did not report for some time. When I finally got to Henry, to explain myself, he was talking with a Congressman. I was a little boy at a wedding.

It went on and on, and on—the heat was overwhelming—the jury took turns, moving from the west side of the courthouse in the morning to the east side in the afternoon. Food was sent in to them, clothing, mattresses, toiletries, and medicines. Outside, in the streets, people were leaning on lampposts, lining roofs. Extra editions of newspapers, hawked among us. "GOSPEL OF GUSH." Henry Ward Beecher is "A dunghill covered with flowers." One editor said, "Mankind fell in Adam, and has been falling ever since, but never touched bottom till it got to Henry Ward Beecher." An English author, Mr. George Meredith, was reported to have found a "sickly snuffiness about the religious fry"; he turned up his British nose at "the amours of costermongers." In my old familiar cafe, over kippers, I read in the *Herald* that "Mr. Beecher presents for the investigation of scientific men a psychological problem that they must despair of solving." I despaired, nibbling on stale toast, of solving anything. Another headline, from Philadelphia, declared:

THE REPUBLIC THREATENED!

After all, Henry had said, "The family is the nation in miniature." Oh, Lord—oh, Family!

Mr. Redpath, a minor attorney for the defense, was so intent on secrecy that he telegraphed Mr. Evarts in Latin.

We wait for the jury. The trial has lasted from January 11, 1875, to July 2, 1875—one hundred and twelve days of formal proceedings. The nation still in the Panic of '73—everywhere, endless fraud and deceit and bullying and blackmail, shady deals—let us, said America, focus on this one. And has taken to it like an anodyne.

The Press became the Judge. From Manhattan to Oregon, Lib is a national heroine—people hate her, people love her, people pity her. She is a "topic." Her published letters are scrutinized over polite dinner parties. The *Times* accusing the *Trib* of big-money fraud, supporting Beecher and maligning Tilton. Oh, we are the headlines we read, the distance between our petty lives and the glittering tribulations of the vigorously talented, mad in their talent. Life declines into literature—and explodes into tabloid. The nation will—give it time, give it time—begin to hunger for hunger—not the birth of tragedy, not the birth of comedy, no, said Tom Beecher, the birth of irony. I had another beer.

And stayed three days at a dingy hotel. It was

my way of disappearing. I sat in the lobby at 4 A.M. Could he not have wanted Lib on the stand because he knew that she did love him? That it would be her love that would betray him? Henry surrounded by adorers. It is terrible to be loved. Could Isabella have sent my letters to Mrs. Stanton or Susan B.—did my letters pass through The Woodhull's fingers? Lib standing up in court, the little sentinel—she is—a *plaything*. I went outside, strolled back to the barn, weltered among the horses, and came out to look at the sunrise. A *plaything*. T. K. Beecher is in a dither, not reliable; he let his brother down, twenty years ago, when he registered his most solemn protest—the fool, the fool! Mr. Evarts had it right when he said, "Men express themselves about their sins generally in inverse ratio to their dessert of blame. Look at it as we may, it is impossible to separate the defendant from his representative character." It is all a morbid jubilee, America Obese.

After eight days and fifty-two ballots, nine to three for acquittal. One juror said that several times they stood eleven to one, and once they had all agreed on Henry's innocence—only to have one juror unfortunately remark that his son had wagered a large sum on the verdict of innocent, and then they split apart again, settling back to nine and three. The numbers beat in my ears. How dreary, how—shabby.

Henry repaired to his summer place. We all saw him off on the train, the depot clamoring with people, babies held up to be kissed. I was bumped to my knees, and the culprit helped me up. Frightened and full of beer, I had an impending sense of disgrace. Henry has won—his demeanor, among so much contradictory evidence, has been the very flag of integrity, rich colors. And it's all the man in the street has to go on.

As the cars move out Henry bellows a benediction: "I am the happiest man in America."

He wasn't. No, not at all—and we began to see the toll that the years had taken. Q: Paralysis? A: A terror of being alone. He immediately swung himself into a lecture tour—through New England, the West, the South. Letters dashed off at hotels in the August twilight:

Temple full, *thousands turned away. Shook hands two hours. Went to Congregational ministers' meeting. Cheering and clapping when I entered. All wept. St. Paul. Royal time.* Laus Deo. *Everywhere this enthusiasm. Madison for nearly two hours I avenged myself upon the audience. Louisville—uncommonly successful trip. Pittsburgh, ah!, the luscious fruits of revenge! The whole slander is burned over like a prairie or an old corn-field. Everywhere upholding the Christian home. I suddenly see the purpose of my life.*

Yes, I thought. Avenge.

Then he was in Indianapolis, lecturing; Indianapolis, where years ago he had won three firsts at the fair—for his squashes, beets, and oyster-plants. The beets weighed from eight to fourteen pounds. And Henry remembered George, his own little boy George. Standing in the snow Henry had laid his son's body into the cold, white grave, his eldest-born son: "I think that if ever one comes near to throwing his soul out of his body—I am in that place. I see the winter down at the very bottom of the grave. The coffin is lowered to its place, and I watch the snowflakes follow it. I have not only lost my child, I have buried him in eternal snow." Now eating blackberries in mountains of cream. There were 4,000 people in Indianapolis when he buried Georgie. Now there are 110,000 citizens. When Henry left—on account of his darling's health—it was on the first train to pass through Indianapolis— the Madison railroad. The Henry Ward Beecher family sat in a wood car, on rigged-up boards set across from side to side, leaving the city where he preached his first real sermon—in a church now long gone. A mighty city now, full of foundries, manufac- tories, a magnificent court-house, wide and fine streets, railroads radiating to every point of the compass.

Theodore Tilton has a new slogan: PULPIT OR PRISON. He got Moulton to sue for libel, but the suit was thrown out of court. Plymouth Church had a permanent "Scandal Bureau"—it went on picnics. Henry wired us, "As long as God himself knows, and my mother knows, I don't care."

So Henry Ward Beecher returned and rested in "Boscobel." A gigantic estate in the Peekskill Val- ley: from the turnpike the private approach runs through a double row of stately maples, three hundred yards to the very doorstep. Sheltered by its own crest from the north winds, its face to the southern sun, the land is encircled by protecting highlands and mountains and low hills and wood- lands. Boscobel spreads up leisurely to the highest point in Westchester County. Over all, rising blue and faint in the distance, the Catskills.

Henry's great plough, pulled by four oxen, drove its steel nose twenty inches down into the earth;

deep drains were sunk across the lower half of the hill to carry off surplus moisture. Wells announced themselves—sudden clear gushing. A hired hand, the foreman, Mr. Thomas Turner, a funny Irishman, down in the mouth, he was always trying to extend the borders of his pea and potato patches, encroaching on Henry's hollyhocks and dahlias. It was not the Beecher-Tilton Trial—it was the Flower-Vegetable Wars. Onions or gladioluses? Lettuce or asters? "Slowly," Henry said, "I am gaining on General Turner."

A clump of Norway spruces fringed on one side with scarlet sumacs; a fine mountain ash; on one of the evergreens an ampelopsis climbing into crimson, something freakish in the way the brilliant vine took liberties with the sober tree, like a child with a solemn grandfather, climbing his shoulders, disarranging his hair, pulling at his sacred spectacles. A votive garden: damask roses, Noisette, Perpetual, Bourbon, China, tea, musk. And on this great stretch of land he would build him a house. As he had designed him a Church, back in Brooklyn, to express and embody his person, so now he would make a cathedral of his country estate—"A house is the shape that a man's thought takes," he said. "The man imagines his life, and interprets in material form who he is. Tommy, I've been stuck for two weeks on the metaphysics of dormer windows." He took great care with the massive fireplaces and great oak beams; the house should be "at once strength and individuality—distinctive repose, imagination held in check by responsibility, the poetic chastened by the practical—typical and unique, thick stone walls and cupolas irrelevating. Huge rooms of display, and little intimate chambers, fireplaces wherever I can fix 'em—my, I remember in Indiana, the thrill I got from my first iron-sided stove."

Looking over his sketches and diagrams I saw the scale he had in mind; I registered my alarm at the expense.

"Oh, Tommy, I am laying up money diligently. I'll meet every bill as it comes due. I take pride in building the house, in *one year,* and earning every penny that pays for it, without a cent of debt—after the world, the flesh, and the devil conspired to put me down!" He heard the fierceness, a throttled rage in his voice, and he softened himself: "Besides, it will give Eunice something to care for." Then he tried to thunder back into the grand: "*Boscobel* will be to house what *Beecher* is to man."

I must have looked at him oddly, for, seeing me, he suddenly looked back—checking a crazy echo.

The great project was completed on schedule; twenty-five boarders was no unusual number. Once, when Henry staged a meeting of the clerical union—at which he performed a Beecher-Tilton trial, doing all the parts!—there were thirty-seven in the castle, in Mecca, sleeping and waking under Boscobel's four great chimneys, three huge verandas yawning to the hills falling away, the largest veranda three stories above the ground, with great scalloped arches. The wallpaper, the frescoes, the ornamental ceramics—vases big enough for a child to hide in.

As for cattle, he started only with Ayrshires, then moved to Jerseys—he loved their beautiful deer-like heads. He had sixteen hundred ornamental shrubs. And Italian bees—which once attacked a calf and almost killed the Irishman. Jerseys and bees—milk and honey! Two canine giants, Bruno and Jack—the one a St. Bernard and the other a Russian bloodhound. Little dogs were named after the paintings on the walls—Dürer and Schoengauer—all bark and wiggle.

Silks, and velvets, and plushes, an opulent giant of a home, in the cottage style, everywhere posts and carved spindles. Cattle, horses, poultry—those sixteen hundred shrubs, they were the very finest in the world, unmatched in splendour save possibly by the Smithsonian. Worship the Great God Size. Barnum! Beecher! Who, in a century full of thunder, is louder?

Eunice was the lady of the house, but Hatty was Henry's partner at croquet. With their mallets, they were Beecher—they always laughed uproariously and showed no mercy. Mischief and violence.

Years before I was born, when Father bought a bale of cotton, because he could pay for it, Roxana spun it, and wove it, and braided it into a carpet, painting bright flowers on the border. A deacon, urged to enter Lyman Beecher's parlor, said, "Can't, 'thout stepping on't!" And asked, "Think you can have all that, and Heaven too?"

Henry can. To his West he sees the greatest exploratory conquest and migration in the history of mankind. Where's Litchfield, where's the place one traces his family back for two centuries? These people, these Americans, they cannot trace their families back twenty years. Community has not passed away; it has been torn away. What laws govern? One hundred forms of denominationalism. How consolidate? It don't matter. It's Boscobel. For thirty years Henry Ward Beecher has been our high priest and millions of Americans believe in his voice—that voice, it burns in my ears, radiates my heart. "I speak on all questions, certainly on politics." Oh, indeed, Henry is the first minister to be seen with Presidents, to campaign vigorously for them, to make a career of being a friend to them. Couldn't have, in 1850. So he took out that oaken pulpit whose function it was to isolate the preacher in lonely magnificence; and in place of the pulpit he put a throne—all right, Tom, an *armchair*—and he led us out of the Old Book into the Promised Land. The heart's blessing in the teeth of luxury. Still he averages one hundred twenty lectures a year, aside from his Sunday sermons. After driving a gent's croquet ball into the creek Henry hops after it, fat, fat, fat and full of fun. He used to lecture against idle amusements, croquet a special danger. Dogmas do not die because they are refuted; they fade away because they are neglected.

He said, "A great middle class has been born." In a spasm of renewed public energy, Henry Ward Beecher started talking all over America—talking to anybody who would hear him, and the folks who showed up were exactly his newly-christened "middle class"—not the old bankers and their ladies; no, these were the boys on salary and their mincing, frugal wives—audiences of clerks and teachers, wanting to know what to do about corruption, the Credit Mobilier, the Whiskey Ring. So Henry preached "The Reign of the Common People," tramping America, away from Plymouth Church over four months every year, covering eighteen states and thirty thousand miles—at a thousand dollars a shot. He said, "In the balmiest days of my life I never had such audiences." And when after a particularly bloody strike, he found out that his middle class was scared to death of the labor unions, he asked, "Is not a dollar a day enough for a man with a wife and six children? Well no, no, not if the man smokes and drinks beer. But is not a dollar a day enough to buy bread with? Water costs nothing, and a man who cannot live on bread and water is not fit to live."

I winced when I read it in the papers, I winced and smelled the ink.

When Father once climbed a huge chestnut tree, growing slant-wise maybe fifty feet over a precipice, our father hurling himself over the abyss, he shook down the nuts to the children, all of us below, looking up to him, and one of the nuts fetched Henry a mighty blow just above the right eye. The blood was profuse. Then we ran home to tell scenes from Scott—Tom doing *The Black Dwarf* and Catharine *The Bride of Lammermoor*.

Now, Catharine has just written another volume, *Letters Addressed to Persons Engaged in Domestic Service*. She will counsel submission until she dies. The masculine imperative has yielded to the Petticoat Brigade, and Caty knows that the females of this country are not wives, not mothers—they are *daughters*. How shall they ever become women? I take Caty's trembling hand in mine, and regard her troubled brow, her ruin of a face—I stand there in my pants and say to myself, Save us from it—oh, save us from Brooklyn Heights, save us from the boys going to the office and the girls being Lib Tilton—God must deliver us, God, or History, or

Biology, Hereditary Habit or a New Social Order—
deliver us, deliver us—

I am weary from standing here beside this large,
slow, ceremonial grief. Henry and his public were
one true love—and they have been everlastingly
harmed. I am standing beside violent pain. Boscobel
is Henry's casket. Color-opiates to be fondled—
fondle trinkets, fondle acres—the brute loneliness—vulgar, demeaning, crushing, extravagant loneliness—and all that weepy yelling:

YOUR WINDOWS ARE AGATES!
YE ARE GODS!

YOSEMITE, I guess. At Henry's seventieth birth-
day dinner, Judge Neilson was a principal speaker;
William Maxwell Evarts is Rutherford B. Hayes's
Secretary of State.

Children, little children in the street sing it:

> *Beecher, Beecher is my name,*
> *Beecher, till I die!*
> *I never kissed Mis Tilton,*
> *I never told a lie!*

We all hear. We all listen. And the chicken who laid
an egg on his head—thus did the admirable creature, the Hen reWard Beecher, oh—"Agonize, *Agonize!*"

Lib and Theodore were the children; Henry, the
Ogre Patriarch. It says Thou shalt not commit
Adultery. It doesn't say Thou shalt not commit
Incest—because, I suppose, "it" doesn't have to. All

stuck there in Brooklyn Heights, virtually in the same house; a crazy wounded family. But I still do not understand Bowen—why did Old Bowen hate Henry so? There is some mystery still in Bowen, who had been contemplating an "awful reality."

When asked, "Is there a Hell to go to?" Henry answered, "Yes, after this one." He didn't lead, and he didn't follow—marching right along beside the troops, exhorting them, cheering them on; their fatigue and eagerness were his, and they saw his as theirs. Or maybe he did not believe in Eternal Damnation because he thought he deserved it. He invested such energy in being a baby, and now he finds himself the chaplain of the 13th Regiment—his white hair flying:

My Dear Colonel,

Your circular is as dark as theology or a wolf's mouth. Shall I wear my resplendent chapeau or my ridiculous cap, in which I look like a pumpkin with a ribbon around it. See you at the armory.

He says, "Christ will throw about me the shield of his righteousness—not because I am not a sinner, but because I am." I asked him which character in Shakespeare he would most like to play. He answered, "Richard the Third." When I pushed him for the reason, he exclaimed, "Oh—to be the *Devil!*" So I asked him which of the founding fathers he would most like to have been—again, his answer was odd: Ben Franklin. So I listened to his views on Franklin, the man who had the key strategies and master-plan for Success in America, the man who knew we wanted a Poor Richard, because we could not tolerate a King, and Old Ben loomed in my mind as the most subtle snake and powerful man of them all. I said, "If he were as big and wise as you make him out to be, Henry, why wasn't he the first President?" Henry looked at me: "Because, Tommy, when George Washington assumed the throne, Old Ben Franklin was *dead*!" And then he laughed—a joke, a rejoinder—but without meanness in it; he seemed to say, I know what it's like to appear a fool, Father always made me feel like one, so now let's laugh.

If Henry Ward Beecher ever had "criminal commerce" it was with a sunset.

Isabella came up to Elmira, to the Gleason Water Cure. We got along, and she was annoyed by my local influence. She had a great program to relieve female troubles: hydropathic gynecology. She was constantly threatening imminent collapse; only her lengthy morning naps seemed to relieve her from nerves and fidgets. Wet packs, sitz baths, injections. She would go into brain fever to save the world through domestic economy and microscopy—Isabella Beecher Hooker, obsessed with the circulation of the blood. Her husband John says 'Gee!' all the time. We do not speak of the old days when she got Mrs. Stanton's and Miss Anthony's assistance—when she threatened to invade Henry's pulpit and read blackmail letters. She talks, in her low pathetic voice, like someone out of Dickens. Not long ago, their daughter, Mary, died of consumption; Isabella would shrink away from her, so as not to contract the disease, and now Isabella cannot get rid of her guilt and panic; she remembers Mary gasping at the last: "Ma, why don't you love me as you use'ter?" That girl's voice howls at Isabella in the night, cries out in the hollow darkness. Isabella sobs. But she is much comforted by Mary's appearance, in a gorgeous vision, on a mountainside.

Hatty, beloved Harriet, much worse. Way back in '49 the cholera epidemic killed the baby, Samuel Charles. In '57 their prize boy, Henry, only nineteen, was drowned on vacation from Dartmouth. While Hatty was taking down Father's autobiography, Fred Stowe, wounded at Gettysburg, became an alcoholic. Old Calvin took him on a long ocean voyage, but could not cure his son of the craving for drink. Fred wrote his mother, "Better far that I should be heare than out in the world disgracing the name you bear it fare more honorable and I hope you will endeavor to forgive what you can neaver forget." Now he has disappeared in San Francisco, dead or shanghaied. And the girl Georgiana is addicted to opiates.

Calvin passed away—across more likely—to hook up with his "visitants." One morning long ago, back in Cincinnati, Calvin did his best to wake up Henry, couldn't, went downstairs with many expressions of disgust; no sooner was he out of the room than Henry sprang up, dressed himself, ran to the Seminary by the back way, and when Professor Stowe entered the room, Henry was sitting demurely at his desk, copying his lesson. Professor was amazed; he rubbed his glasses, peered again. *Visitants*.

All around me now I see ugly furniture, this craze for black walnut copies of the Gothic. I see, as well, coarseness, the domestic signature of the Erie Gamble and Tweed's Gang—America swollen. The paternity of the boy Ralph—an *ass* out of the pit—it is all, it is all—Shame. All of us Beechers, all eleven of Father's children—Beecher until we die—our victories and defeats, all so public. The borough politics of God. Father could say of one of Henry's sermons, "It has no doctrine, no edification in it; it is all moonshine—and I despise it!"; but, if someone should praise a Henry Ward Beecher sermon, Father would shake his finger and say, "Remember, if it warn't for me, you never would have had him!" And it is one of Father's achievements to have kept us so close, all his life, and beyond, into ours—all of us subject to his furious appeal and the possessive torrent of his nature. We cannot escape him, his cajolery, his caresses, his battering and pampering. He so relished our every achievement, took so intimately to heart our woes, so gloried in our fame—we are his.

And then Grover Cleveland was discovered to be an Adulterer. So Henry became Chief Mugwump; he campaigned as if he were twenty-one, not seventy-one, shouting, shouting down the crowds and bringing back all his early triumphs and all his recent pain. He said, "I have tasted blood, and I have to go on tasting it." We told him, soberly, that once again he was rushing upon self-destruction. He replied in his usual figure; he was giving help "as a mother gives her breast to her child." His language ballooned out of his conscious control; seeing that "Slander takes on the guilt of the crime alleged," he smashed "the cockatrice's eggs brooded and hatched by brash and credulous politicos. The accusers could not go to Mr. Cleveland with honest inquiry, so they opened their ears to the harlot and the drunkard. To turn the White House into a salacious whispering-gallery—the plagues of Egypt, the land swarms with vermin, frogs slime our bread troughs, and lice crawl about our beds." Some applauded, some hooted, some howled. Mr. Mark Twain said that it was an act of courage for a reputable citizen even to vote for Cleveland, and there was Henry, weighty Henry, on platform after platform, rousing the multitudes. All his life he has thrown himself on what he was most afraid of. Henry said, "I am opposing the party whose cradle I rocked because I will not carry its coffin to the grave. Mr. Cleveland's public life is above suspicion, and some have suggested profligacy in his private life. His opponent's scruples are in reverse. Therefore, let us elect Mr. Cleveland to the public office which he is so admirably qualified to fill, and remand Mr. Blaine to the private life which he is so eminently fitted to adorn!"

The night before the last rally I was with Hatty, and she showed me a letter Mr. Blaine had written her:

I was never more surprised in my life than when I found your gifted and eloquent brother opposing me. We had been friends for so many years that it came upon me as a sore disappointment. Please tell the Rev. H.W.B. that he should not turn his back on his own connections.

Hatty asked me, "What, Tom, do you think of that?"

"I think Blaine should have known better."

"Yes. Entreaty of a sinister kind. Flattery and threat. I fear I didn't see that immediately. I told Henry it was an honor. He said, 'After seventy, honors are at a discount.'"

"Good for Henry."

Hatty smiled, frightened. "All of us urging him to stay clear of it. 'Remember Tilton—spare yourself.'"

"He won't."

"No," she said, "he won't."

We looked at each other, my half-sister and I. She said, "Are we to witness a disaster or a triumph?"

Both, I thought, and took us to the cab. We went together to the final rally for Grover Cleveland. There—at the Brooklyn Academy of Music—I saw that Henry's great defense, his great escape—his laughter—it was all becoming cruel. After he had led a parade through a profusion of torches, the ground aflame in solid avenues of fire—Henry stood on the stage, and boomed:

When in the gloomy night of my own suffering, when I sounded every depth of sorrow, I vowed that I would never suffer a brother to go unfriended, should a like serpent see a way to crush him. That oath I now regard! Family and friends counsel me to prudence lest I stir again my own griefs. No! I will not be prudent. I will interpose a shield of well-placed confidence between Governor Cleveland and the base obscenities hurled at him by a herd of dolts and mean-spirited scoundrels!

Henry thundered down the crowd, he had them in the palm of his hand, he had them all in his hands, and he just screamed at 'em: "If every man in New York state tonight who has broken the seventh commandment voted for Cleveland, he would be elected by a 200,000 majority!"

Holding Hatty's fierce hand, I heard the mob let out a gorgeous roar, and I peered up at Henry, Henry just walking around, Henry smiling at them, their volcanic response—and he threw his hat—he threw his grand old hat to them—and they caught it, and they sent it all around the auditorium, his hat was not exactly in the ring—except in the ring of fire—Henry reminding the nation of his own dark night—Henry who was so bashful as a boy that to walk into a room where "company" was assembled, and be natural, was as impossible—as impossible as it would be to fly!

Cold Tom escorted Harriet Beecher Stowe back to Columbia Heights, and we lived through the reception, and at last I cuddled down into the bottom of my little anteroom bed; I closed shop, closed out the world, and dreamed, dreamed of the ride to the Canal Boat . . . boyhood . . . October . . . trunk tumbled out one side as Tom tumbles in the other . . . reverse order, tumble Tom out, trunk in. At length, all aboard, and Father drives out of the yard, yelling for us to hold on, one rein in the right hand and the other in the left, an apple in each, Father biting them alternately, raising and lowering the reins like threads on a loom. At full canter, carriage bouncing and bounding over the stones, Father telling Charley how to get the harness mended, and showing Henry the true doctrine of original sin, the trunk, apples flying, a piece of apple on Father's chin—hurrah!—we make the boat.

I wake up. Eunice is in Florida; the rest of the house is still asleep. It is 6 A.M. I quietly descend the stairs, sit in the kitchen, and drink tea. I have not a single idea. I won't plan—I won't hope—I won't fear. This world is a gloomy place. I give it up. I have no part in it. One can only endeavor to bind up its gashes, shine into its darkness, keep from its evil, prophesy Heaven and wait—wait—singing songs in the night.

Well, I had to get to work. I used to be afraid I would forget things; now I can't stop remembering them. I am living in the new age all right, but with a throwback set of innards.

In Elmira Thomas Kinnicut Beecher preached to the daughters of Mr. Clemens. Appropriate, for I had officiated at the nuptials, when Sam Clemens took Olivia Langdon as his bride. Mark Twain, such a splendid man—doomed, blasted, most amusing, coarse to the core, angry, his anger like a beacon at night, oh, such glorious anger—or is it shame, is that shame too?

Our Jamesy died. He drank himself to death. In his last letter to me he wrote, "Tom, I think the Seaman's Bethel, Canton, is the right place for me. I was fit for Crusoe's Island, or the Golden Age, or a Moravian Brotherhood—but this is the Age of Upstarts!" Woebegone Jamesy. Did he see the full blaze of the Shekinah? "Bitterness"—a dead letter to "Tenderness." Forgiveness howling at Forebearance.

Henry took Eunice on his great, last voyage to England. Henry muttered, "Father wore out three wives—one's enough to wear me out." June 19, the *Etruria* sailed. Just off Liberty Island, the excursion steamer, *Grand Republic*, with three thousand of us aboard, came alongside the *Etruria* to pay a farewell tribute. "Hail to the Chief," reciprocal whistle salutes, and the Plymouth choir singing the Doxology. The Beecher stateroom embanked in flowers; twenty homing pigeons were provided so that precious messages could swiftly return from the open sea. And Henry broadcast his great theme: "The most beautiful thing that lives on this earth is not the child in the cradle, sweet as it is. It is not ample enough. It has not history. It is all prophecy. Let me see a great nature, that has gone through sorrows, through fire, flood and thunder, enlarging, growing finer, and finally gentle, with great knowledge of the long struggle—let me see such a one stand at the end of life, as the sun stands on a summer afternoon just before it goes down. Is there anything on earth so beautiful as a rich, ripe, large, glowing and glorious heart? No nothing."

That hot June evening, after the *Etruria* had sailed out of sight, I was on the train back to Elmira, my sky the forbidding slate that hangs over the Chemung Valley. No visions for Cold Tom. But when the train reached Elmira, I did see the world, I, Thomas Kinnicut Beecher. I had my Aurora Borealis, my black bird in the orange thunderheads. And, wouldn't you know? I had mine at night. That June night, especially muggy, the temperature at one hundred and the humidity up there too; I went out into my yard to find the fireflies—fireflies everywhere, thousands of them, not lying low in the grass, they were going up high, into my Japanese Maple, my dour elms, my leaning sycamores, a million of them, tiny lights, flashing a profusion of musical code. I trapped one, cupped it in my hand, its lemon silver—not gold—in my hand. And then I let it go, and it sped off in silent winking darkness, joined the city of lights in the trees—and I thought life was music—higher, speeding into foliage, until all my yard was living, living light, light loud as sound—

TKB, fond old fellow, end as a Rhapsodist! Forever I will be Henry Ward Beecher's brother, Harriet Beecher Stowe's brother, Lyman Beecher's son. It matters little; it matters not at all. Over in the long grass by the stream, my tricycle—used now so little, so infrequently, that the grass has grown up to meet the wheels, the weeds all over it, my trike incandescent with fireflies. I sat upon it there, with grandiose chiming radiance in my spokes, careering on my steed, for the ecstasy, for the hell of it, sitting on my great iron and rosewood vehicle, singing Father's favorite fiddle tune: "Go to the Devil and Shake Yourself."

Great God, Father was there in the kitchen, watching the children being bathed, and he put Catharine's two-year-old head under water, just— just to see what she would do!

Why, I think I exist! Crazy Sally sitting on the stairs in Park Church, her lower teeth gouging quietly at her upper lip: "I better say something. I *am* saying something. Shouldn't talk in meeting. Tsk-tsk, I am saying something. Better not talk in meeting. But I said that too! Mustn't talk in meeting—there I go again!" Crazy Sally stinks, and makes us rejoice: Crazy Sally's as gamey as a wonderful meal of seafood, orange and ivory crab's legs, Sally desperate and ill and gallant—

Caty's head, Lyman Beecher slammed it under water, just to see what she would do!

In the long grass and ragweed—the wheel in a wheel, the damn fool, he'll get killed driving like that—oh, I do believe I am the last Calvinist in the family. My tone is all negation and irony—well, we are all lost children. Let us be gentle, forgiving, patient, and kind. The world is our parish. We cannot see the want of proportion between ends contemplated and means employed. By and by our elder brother will come to lead us home.

A chariot of fire, a tricycle of fireflies.

And I—I was father's favorite. "Mother, I am a hero!"

When my father couldn't remember my mother—when my father referred to my mother as Roxana—not Harriet Porter—but she was my mother, mine, Henry Ward's wicked step-mother, whose kiss was frost—but, oh, when I was a little boy preparing for bed, my father would take down his fiddle, and—off with his shoes—he loved to dance in his socks, partly for the pleasure of wearing through the heels so that she would have to mend them—and Father would love his jig, love the holes, love the violin, love life, love the Devil, love God—our father down there (our father who kept a great mound of sand in the cellar, just so's he could go down and shovel it around)—one night when I was a little boy, my mother, as she was saying goodnight to me, my mother, Harriet Porter, her hair braided and combed up back, she stood there beside my bed, she was just standing there and hearing my father wildly fiddling below—and my mother tilted her head, as if to say, 'What's the use?—oh, what is the use in fighting him *always*'—and Mother, slowly, rhythmically, began to dance, holding her arms out, my own mother, wheeling and gliding about that upstairs room, gliding across its bare floor—

Henry Ward Beecher, in his seventy-fourth year, died on March 9, 1887. Stricken on the seventh, he remained able to talk and move about for two days, then passed on in his sleep. No paralysis. His last public act was a letter about the Strauss Ministry nomination; Henry wrote to President Cleveland:

This bitter prejudice against Jews which obtains in many parts of Europe ought not to receive any countenance in America. It is because Strauss is a Jew that I would urge his appointment. It is a fit recognition of this remarkable people, who are becoming large contributors to American prosperity, and whose intelligence, morality, and large liberality in all public measures for the welfare of society deserve recognition.

Well, there's a sting in there, but we haven't time for it, certainly not when a prominent rabbi proclaims, "Anti-Semitism has threatened to take hold of certain circles in America, and Beecher, Beecher almost alone among the Christian clergy, championed the cause of the Jews." And then the tributes came pouring in—first from Edwin Booth (who better to be first?), Charles Parnell, seven Civil War generals (both Union and Confederate), Andrew Carnegie, Louis Pasteur, and Alexander Graham Bell. The Negro clergy of New York City marched en masse. But the Chicago Congregationalists voted not to send a testimonial—no, we "Christians" do not cease hating each other at the grave.

On the train from Elmira to New York I traced the sweating windows for the last time I saw Henry alive. It was at Boscobel, the previous Fourth of July. We were sitting on a lower veranda drinking champagne, watching the children, a half-dozen of them bobbing for apples. Henry (just itching for the sunset, so's he could be Chief Pyrotech, his rockets ready for our country's 110th), Henry suddenly turned to me, his jowls shaking: "Do you remember Father's apple-peeling bees, Tommy? See the children there now—doesn't it remind you of Father's wassails of theology? Q: Is sin born in the nature of a child? Q: Does a child have a nature? Q: Is sin action or thought? Oh, don't you remember, Tommy?— father and son, peeling the apples, debating the nature of right action anterior to saving change." Henry loved the words—he finally loved the words, for they were color-opiates, and he stared at their ever-lasting beauty. Henry was stunned, stunned sick and coming up coherent: "Is conversion the act of choice on the sinner's part or an irresistible influence exerted upon him *ab extra?*" He pointed toward the children; with his crystal glass he looked at them, looked through the champagne at a darting renegade, as if a child were a syllable. He yawned, and fondled himself, though he was in some kind of dull pain, dull and deep. Trying not to show it. "That 'smart' one there, Tommy, she's a darling—Agatha—I was sitting with her by the apple barrel this morning and I remembered it all, Tommy, those wonderful times with Father—and I asked her, my peeling-knife poised in the air—old Grampa asked her, 'What, Aggie-love, are the four great religions of the world?' Oh, Tommy, she's nine years old. She looked at Fearsome Grandfather and said, straight out, 'Christianity, the Catholics—Jewish—and Norway.'" Henry shook with laughter in his chair, his wicker throne, shook himself out of slow pain into wonder. He was always so lovely with children. "Christianity, the Catholics—Jewish—and Norway."

I take the ferry to Brooklyn. One hears that Victoria Woodhull got loose from Colonel Blood somewhere along the line; she accused him of—adultery. Victoria, the Crisis Hussy, is never happy unless the world is in trouble; she went to England for a while; they say that she is coming back to us, to rehabilitate the ancestral home of George Washington. Her Zulu Maud gives Shakespeare readings. At the time of The Great Scandal, Thomas Nast put cloven hooves and bat wings on The Woodhull—but she wasn't Mrs. Satan, she wasn't a vulgar adventuress, I don't know what she was. Theodore Tilton lives in Paris now, a boulevardier writing verses and drinking absinthe at the Café de la Regence. At the trial he said, "I am a weak man, supposed to be strong; mockery breeds agony in me, I cannot endure mockery." And Mr. Evarts said, "Few of us assembled here thrive on it." Lib Tilton, Lib is still in New York, but allows no newspapers in her house; not that she could read them—for she is blind. Cared for by her daughter. Lib blind! What does she see in her darkness?

Plymouth, a garden. According to Henry's wishes, Plymouth Church was not encumbered with anything black. Bowers of roses and smilax and evergreen, festoons of laurel from the four corners of the gigantic ceiling, French and Eucharis roses. Eighty thousand passed by—four-fifths of them women. All this, and Boscobel too—it is some recompense, some answer to that time in the White Water Valley when he would pluck rare blossoms and stroll through the muddy streets, dispensing floral edification.

In that house on Columbia Heights, after the great Plymouth service, the family was dispersed among the rooms—released from our immense living in public, alone with each other. I was sitting in the library with Hatty and Edward. And then I heard—I heard—

Old Bowen! No, I had never, never understood Mr. Bowen. The man who called Henry from Indianapolis to Brooklyn, the Captain of Empire who had presided over the founding and the building of the church, Henry Bowen, publisher of the *Independent* and the *Christian Union*—this immensely powerful man who had suddenly turned against Henry, turned against his own hand-picked man, so inexplicably, so terribly. Hatty and Edward and I, in our slow conversation now, we paused carefully at some little *memento mori* of the great scandal, the "Beecher-Tilton Trial" that had held America breathless for six months back in '75; Edward remarked, sighing, "No issue! Henry's whole life was great issues, and that thing had none of 'em, no great issue—"

Harriet turned on Edward, with a fierceness, "No great issue?" she snarled. "It is the great issue! It is the greatest issue of all, Eddie—who we *are* to each other." And Hatty began, on the spot, to weep. She stood there grinding her soul in tears. Her woe was an engine, and she tottered out of the room.

That was when Edward told me, staring at his wooden leg. Edward, as if he were defending himself, a Christian soldier, in that dry, non-committal voice, that quiet voice: apprised of the circumstances, oblivious to the shadow. He told it to me, he gave it to me like a dusty law book, he told me the story: when Henry Bowen's wife lay dying, she spoke to him, she told him that she and Henry Ward Beecher—she had—and they had—and Bowen's wife was given, by Henry Ward Beecher, a key, a key to his private room behind the throne, behind the demolished pulpit, a key to his anteroom, the place where Henry had Sarah the slave-girl wait that day, a key to his own special room, the treasures of his imagination and his chaise-lounge. Then, months later, one day Mrs. Bowen saw another woman at the door, putting in *her* key, and—and Lady Bowen was so hurt, in her guilt and longing, the dark flush of betrayal—so she told her husband, the death-bed confession of the Romances, as her immortal soul died away from her consumptive body, as she witnessed the rapture of the King—she told the true secret—

And Old Bowen brooded over the awful reality. In the closed coach, stalled in the *cortège,* sitting there down under the roof of his black cab in the rain, sitting there in the dismal public rain and in his own loss, staring at his black ring, twisting it, Old Bowen brooded over the awful reality.

In the house on Columbia Heights, Edward's meadow-smooth, stupid voice, telling me that—the details were sordid palaver and Spectre Evidence. Edward, the President of Illinois College, Emeritus, telling me that some Dean's wife is always taking a fancy to a green Prof., it's the way of the world, Brother Eddie picking his wooden leg, Edward's permanent delirium of Sabbaths—and I felt my marrow creep, I felt it in my vague, erratic hands and throbbing legs, and then in my whole body. That is why my feeling for Henry has been so unclear—it is because I am in the grip of him—I have been, all my life, as only a younger and half-brother can be; now Henry's organ voice rose out of Edward's dull recitation, Henry's voice ringing in my ears, his voice rebounding from the blue and burgundy of the Persian carpet, a great bell of voice, a blinding, blinding voice, it is why I always hated the world when I was around him—and The Woodhull was right, Henry was not unfaithful to the old doctrines, he was guilty of infidelity to the new—and Victoria Woodhull's Free Love will conquer all, we won't know how to care anymore—did Henry care?—did he? as he was taking off Lib Tilton's underclothes, laying those precious garments beside *Norwood,* breathing in her neck, touching her dainty free bosoms—a swoon of hurt—his big voice whispering in her ears—Lib's undergarments, her petite, naked, sweet, sweet body—he had seen her grow up from a child, from a bright little girl who played with his own bright little girl—Lib was just, just like his daughter—and he knew, he knew that is why she could not appear on the stand—he knew he was guilty, guilty of the High Crime and Misdemeanor— Erotic Dwelling, Nest-Hiding—and now it is all so clear, grief upon grief—

Harriet sank all her savings into protecting Henry, protecting our darling Henry, not because he was innocent, but because he was guilty—because we are Beecher—Beecher, Beecher, 'til I die— Henry pushing himself, bashfully, wise, father, Romeo, onto the—red lounge!—"A good woman, my dear, can save a bad man, but no good man ever saved a bad woman"—what did he say?—(Well, in court he said Adam and Eve were guilty of inexperience! I should strike my forehead and laugh, for I am a Man of the World! At least the eminent tricyclist of Elmira.) Henry guilty, Henry knowing it, Henry living it—living it in the Dionysean brevity, the sacred hours, and over the sober years—The Brain sends out its legions, The Heart sends back its mob. Carnage and Administration. I've missed life. And I'm damned glad of it. "Forgiveness." "Punishment." Only words have meaning—isolated words. The age of novels is over. Narrative is Curio. My big brother disinvented Hell in his lifetime. My big brother did not call me Cold Tom—he always called me Tommy—in front of people, even when there were no people.

O Moses! And Edward looking at me now with the eyes of history: intimacy as relic. My own eyes wandered up the stairway clogged with lillies and jammed with great bouquets. Harriet! Oh, our Hatty—women are not a different sex, they are a different race—

I staggered out to the porch, and fell into a large rain-stained chair. I sat there, hearing Hatty upstairs and Edward's silence in the haunted library. To Hear Beecher—To Hear Beecher.

And Eunice was standing there, at the door into the kitchen. She had heard Hatty, heard Edward, and now Eunice in black not for Henry, but as she always is, and has been for years, all in black, her radiant white hair like a crown, Eunice came slowly out into the sharp cold of the porch. She said, "All women, I am told, marry Gods, but sadly consent afterwards to live with men. For me it was the reverse."

I heard her words, heard them again. Eunice Bullard has been Henry Ward Beecher's wife, and she never let Theodore Tilton into her house. "The Griffin" knew. Henry knew she did. She bore their children, and she buried them. She bore Henry, buried him. She herself had written, "I can but look with longing on the promised land, the storehouse of poetry and romance; I may not unlock the gates and enter in." Eunice, the author of *All Around The House, or How To Make Homes Happy*. She had watched Henry lie in front of a fire, turning it into a hunting scene—a faint line of blue gas, issuing at little intervals from cracks, those were rabbits or foxes; then, from the end of a log a flame like a hound, leaping over, catches the foxes, racing around the whole front end and disappearing around the corner. Henry looks up; he meets the eyes of his life's partner, "The Griffin."

Race, for reassurance, to Plymouth!

Standing there, Eunice said to me, "I live in the past, Tom. Over and over. Every little while when talking most cheerfully, such a flood sweeps over me that I am constantly on the watch, lest I lose my self-control."

She sat down. "That scandal gave him, at home, a colder, more abrupt way of speaking—less tender and loving. I missed it more than tongue could tell. It is not strange, but I longed for the old tones."

I said, "It would be strange—if that struggle should not have changed him."

"Much changed him. It was very bitter to have him go away, after the trial—worse than it was years before. And while we were under that mysterious cloud, and feeling its cruelty—I was in danger far worse than death."

"Yes."

"My love for him would grow cold and waver. If his heart had not changed woefully, he would not—he could not have subjected me to the torture of that terrible long time." Her big hands fussed with her great skirts. "Of course I wanted to have the children move in, and with their families, but—but Henry put it to me as an economy measure—I lost my place—I lost my usefulness. I told him, and he took me with him on tour. But I couldn't bear to watch him. It broke my heart, to see his broken heart. I lost the last rag of hope—" Then, suddenly, she laughed. "When he came back from a session with President Lincoln, he told me, he was so excited, like a boy, he said, 'Honest Abe told me three stories, two of which I have forgotten, and the third was improper.'" The old woman smiled. "I said to him, 'Tell me, Henry, how is it that you remember the bad one?'"

Q: Why is Eunice talking?
A: Because Henry's dead. Because the children, her lost children, are grave-robbers. Wait—

wait and hear her outraged grief about the silver—the silver with the inlay initials.

"Once, on tour, I did not behave properly at all. It was my fault, in Milwaukee. I knew he was in pain, but I began to lurch for my own life—oh, Tom—" She composed herself. "He wrote to a Bishop who had inquired about my welfare. Henry wrote to him, 'Her morbid craving for sympathy over fictitious woes seems like the appetite of an inebriate.'"

I saw it in Henry's handwriting, and I saw her eyes discovering it—fictitious woes in Milwaukee.

"The appetite of an inebriate! And all I ever tasted was Spruce Beer." Her eyes came over to me. "Tom, you have been inebriated. What is it like?"

"Oh—it's an adventure—an adventure of Grace and Condescension."

She stared at me. "No, truly?"

I felt assaulted. I stammered, "Well, it's like the past."

She let a silence ride, just between us. And then she said, "Perhaps that is why I have been incapable of—I have always known, or have always told myself, that tomorrow is not stronger than the past, but tomorrow will always be there. Well, I suppose that's not a very new idea."

In the library, worlds away, Edward awoke from some little slumber he'd sneaked; he shouted, "Everybody go to Church and leave an old man alone?"

Eunice heard it. I made a motion with my head.

"Wait—Tom—I want to show you something." Eunice went into the library, and I could hear her calming Edward, finding his leg.

When she came back she was all alive: "Here it

is, it's the last letter, the very last letter Henry wrote to me." She had cherished it, clearly; it was carefully pressed. I held it on my knee.

O cruel woman! Will not forty years of incessant assailing suffice? Not a bone in my body that you have not broken; not a method of mutilation that you have not tried. You have plunged me down ravines, pitched me over precipices, drowned me, burned me, torn me asunder. I have lost innumerable arms, legs, and feet. I go limping, handless, toward I know not what dire future.

Handless. My brain went a little wild; almost involuntarily I said, "What a poet he was!"

"Oh my no."

I looked up.

"In the trial, that terrible trial, I saw it. Standing by him, I still lost him. Henry didn't want me—he wanted America." Eunice was in a far place, and she whispered, "I am the widow of a household word."